Other Books By

David Kerr Chivers

Alien World

Rudi for President

Metacomet's War

A Novel of King Philip's War

David Kerr Chivers

iUniverse, Inc.
New York Bloomington

Metacomet's War

A Novel of King Philip's War

iUniverse books may be ordered through booksellers or by contacting:

iUniverse
1663 Liberty Drive
Bloomington, IN 47403
www.iuniverse.com
1-800-Authors (1-800-288-4677)

ISBN: 978-1-4401-0404-6 (pbk)
ISBN: 978-1-4401-0405-3 (ebk)

Library of Congress Control Number: 2008939115

Printed in the United States of America

To Marie,
and to

Nate and Adam

Plymouth - June, 1675

The air had a lingering crispness on this June day, and farmers worried of an unusually late frost, some even covering their house gardens with a heavy layer of straw. But other than taking time for this small precaution, no one did anything but talk of the Trial.

Twelve men of Plymouth, men of solid character, men such as Nathaniel Winslow, Andrew Ridge, and Benjamin Higgins, were brought together as a jury to determine the truth. Along with the twelve jurors sat a smaller, auxiliary jury of six Indians to hear the charges and consult as necessary, as was the custom when the person on trial was an Indian.

Three prisoners, shackled, looking gaunt and weary from their imprisonment in the cramped jail, were herded into the courtroom. The clerk stood.

"Tobias, Wampapaquan, and Mattashinnamy, it is said that you did with joint consent upon the 29th of January past, at a place called Assowamsett Pond, willfully and of set purpose, with malice aforethought and by force of arms, murder John Sassamon, another Indian, by laying violent hand on him, striking him, or twisting his neck until he was dead, and to hide and conceal this murder, at the time and place aforesaid, did cast his dead body through a hole of the ice into the said pond." The clerk looked around the room, trying to impress the audience with his solemn demeanor before resuming his seat.

The judge, dressed in his dark robes of office, looked to the prosecutor.

"Present your case," he said simply.

"Good gentlemen of the jury," the prosecutor began, "it was in the fall when the Indian John Sassamon came to the leaders of Plymouth with disturbing news. Philip, sachem of the Wampanoags, was organizing the

Indians for war on the English. Sassamon was known to be in the highest councils of Philip, and his warning taken seriously.

"In January, just a few short weeks after bringing this warning, he is found dead, murdered. The evidence you shall hear will convince you that these three men, known to be among Philip's closest counselors, were the cause of that murder." He turned away from the jury and motioned to the guard placed at the rear of the room.

"I would call the Indian known as David to the stand!"

Heads turned as a small, olive colored man in an ill fitting jacket and trousers walked to the seat reserved for witnesses. He looked around the room nervously, never having been in so formal a setting before.

"Please sir," the prosecutor said as courteously as possible, "Tell us what happened this past January."

"I found his body," the Indian said in halting English. The courtroom was silent as they waited for more.

"How did you come to find it?" the prosecutor prodded.

"I found it on the pond."

"Assowamsett Pond?"

"Yes. I saw his hat upon the ice. And as I came close, a gun. I looked around, but saw no one." Now the Indian relaxed, caught up in his well rehearsed story. "I saw a hole in the ice a few feet away. I went to it and reached into the water. It took a few moments, but then I grabbed onto something hard. I took hold and pulled. I pulled it to the hole. I saw it was a foot."

The onlookers gasped, and there was a rush of whispers. A call for order silenced them. The prosecutor told the Indian David to continue.

"I called for help from a companion. We pulled the body through the hole and brought it up on the ice."

The prosecutor interrupted to add to the dramatic effect.

"Who, pray tell, was the body?"

"John Sassamon, the Indian."

"Order. I will have order in the room," the judge boomed, quelling murmurs that erupted at the mention of Sassamon's name.

"What condition was the body in when you found it?" the prosecutor questioned, relishing the words as he asked them.

"Cold," the Indian said, then winced at the small titter of laughter and prosecutor's scowl.

"Were there bruises?" the prosecutor asked in his firmest voice.

"Yes," came the meek reply.

"Of what nature?"

"There were bruises on his head and shoulders. And his head hung sideways, as if the neck was not holding it."

"Could you tell whether the bruises had been inflicted by the ice, or by a man?"

"No."

"What did you do then?"

"I buried him. A Christian burial." The Indian said this proudly. He was a Christian himself, one of several thousand "Praying Indians" scattered throughout the colony.

"Thank you. That is all."

"You may step down, unless the defendants have questions for you," the judge said. The three prisoners stared straight ahead, making no sign.

The judge nodded to the witness, who didn't hesitate in scurrying from his seat and out the door.

The next witness was a dull-eyed examiner sent by the authorities to dig up Sassamon's body and report upon it. He stated his firm conviction that the bruises and broken neck were not accidental, but the result of another person.

"Do you have an opinion as to the person responsible?"

"Yes I do. Tobias, the Indian."

"And on what evidence is that opinion based?"

"When examining the body, I had Tobias brought in to see it."

"And what was the result?"

"As Tobias approached, the blood began to flow from the body, and continued to do so until Tobias has been removed from its presence." The courtroom nodded their approval. It was well known that if one person killed another, the body of the victim would bleed if approached by the murderer.

"Thank you sir."

"Questions?" the judge asked the Indians. They remained silent.

"I ask that Patuckson the Indian be brought to the stand," the prosecutor said. The courtroom rustled as men pulled themselves up in their seats, eager to see and listen to this other Indian, rumored to be an eyewitness to the murder, although only lately found.

The Indian, tall, well featured, and well dressed in new breeches and jacket, took the stand. His manner stood in sharp contrast to David's. He was composed and in control of himself. Tobias, in his chains, eyed him suspiciously.

"Now Patuckson," the prosecutor began. "Where were you on the day in question?"

"I was upon a hillside, overlooking Assowamsett Pond. I was resting from my travels."

"Did you see anyone on the pond?"

"Yes. I saw Sassamon. He was fishing through the ice."

"Was anyone else there?""

"At first, no. But soon he was joined by Tobias. They talked."

"What did they say?"

"I could not hear. But they started to push each other. It was then that the other two joined Tobias."

"What did they do?"

"They grabbed Sassamon by the arms. They continued to argue. Then Tobias stepped forward and grabbed Sassamon's head, twisting it until the bones cracked. Sassamon went limp. The three of them pushed the body to the hole and tried shoving it through, but the hole was not large enough. So one of them took out a knife and chopped the hole larger, until they were able to push the body out of sight. Then they left."

"And you saw all this clearly?"

"Yes."

"Why did you not report it to the authorities at the time?" The prosecutor smiled slightly. The last question had been his own idea.

"I was afraid the same fate that had befallen Sassamon might soon befall me, should I speak."

"Are you still afraid?"

"Yes."

The judge had to yell for order several times before the courtroom quieted. Patuckson's coming forward only after so many months confirmed the danger Philip's followers posed. They were ruthless killers, even of their own.

The prosecutor sat down, satisfied his contribution to justice had been made.

"Do the defendants wish to question the witness on what he saw?"

Tobias arose, marshaling all the strength within him. "I would question him on the amount of debt he owes to me."

The prosecutor jumped to his feet, but the judge was ahead of him.

"That has no bearing on the case. Stay within the facts of the day. Do you wish to question him regarding what he saw that day at Assowamsett Pond?"

Tobias stood very still for a few moments, and courtroom eyes grew strained staring at him, trying to read his thoughts.

"No," he said simply, and sat down.

"Any further witnesses?"

"None," the prosecutor stated.

"And you?" the judge asked, looking at the three Indians still shackled.

"None that could make a difference to this court," Tobias said, his contempt evident in his sneer. To the courtroom observers, it only confirmed he was nothing more than a cold, ruthless savage.

"Very well. The jury will deliberate. The court is adjourned until such time as a verdict is decided." As the judge left the bench, several town stalwarts struggled up to the rail to congratulate the prosecutor, but he waved them away.

"There can be no congratulations," he said with due modesty, "unless and until the jury sees fit to return a verdict of guilty." He picked up the papers he had in front of him and walked out the side entrance. The prisoners were hustled out the other entrance, back to the dirt-floored jail where they would wait until a verdict had been reached.

"What say ye, gentlemen of the jury?"

Edward Sturgis rose, holding a slip of paper in his hand, on which he had scrawled out the finding.

"We of the jury one and all, both English and Indian, do jointly and with one consent agree upon a verdict - that Tobias and his son Wampapaquan, and Mattashinnamy, the Indians who are the prisoners, are guilty of the blood of John Sassamon, and were the murderers of him according to the bill of indictment."

The judge nodded in solemn agreement, and spoke above the courtroom murmurs.

"The jury having reached its verdict, this court shall now pass sentence. The prisoners shall be taken to the place of execution forthwith and there be hanged by the head until their bodies are dead."

As the three Indians stood silently by, the ropes were hastily prepared and a log bench set under a rail to serve as a gallows. The ropes were tossed over the rail, and the Indians made to step onto the bench, where the nooses were fit snugly onto their necks.

Tobias and Mattashinnamy remained quiet and defiant. But Wampapaquan let out a small whimper as the noose was cinched up tight. A stern look from his father rebuked him into silence, but his eyes remained wide. Onlookers who had pushed in close saw tears forming.

"Do you have any last words?"

Again Wampapaquan began to speak, but was silenced by his father's hard gaze.

With a brief nod from the overseer, the bench was kicked out from underneath them. The ropes went taut and for a brief moment all three men hung in the air. Then with a crash Wampapaquan's body fell to the ground, the noose still around his neck, dangling strands of rope hanging from the rail. He writhed on the ground, gasping for precious breaths from the noose still pushing into his neck. He looked wildly up into the sunlight, seeing only the dark, still outlines of his father and Mattashinnamy.

Hands grabbed him, pushed him down, holding him still, making it even harder to breath. But then a hand on his throat loosened the hemp threads and glorious air rushed into his lungs. He sputtered and coughed, and then retched.

"Shall we prepare another rope?" he heard a man ask.

"No!" Wampapaquan managed to yell between coughs. "No!" He inhaled deeply, regaining his voice. "I will confess. I was there. But I did not kill Sassamon. They did," he said, motioning wildly up at the two bodies suspended above him. "I wanted no part, but they forced me. I could not tell before in fear of my life. But I tell you now it was them. I had nothing to do with it."

The magistrate signaled to put Wampapaquan onto his feet.

"Take him back to the jail, there to await his fate. His confession may yet save him from the hangman's noose. Go. Take him away."

Wampapaquan was shoved roughly from behind. He stumbled onto his knees, his face hitting dangling feet. He looked up into the eyes of his father, still open in death, staring accusingly down at him.

"Forgive me, my father," Wampapaquan whispered softly, "but I have no wish to die." He was hauled up onto his feet again and forced down the road back to his jail. Behind him the heads of the two dead Indians were cut from their bodies, and placed on poles in the town square for all to look on, and be warned.

A few days later, his full confession having been heard and duly recorded, Wampapaquan was taken out and shot.

Three Toes moved warily to my feet, placing her muzzle on my leg and looking mournfully up at me. I looked down, smiled sadly, and stroked my dog's soft fur with one hand, while slipping some meat scraps from my bowl into her mouth. She chewed noisily on the rare treat, given to her only when I was alone in the wigwam, as I was now. I sighed heavily. I am Metacomet, although the English know me as King Philip. Philip was the name the English had given me, and for years I had lived with it, for a time I had even cherished it. But no more. Now I again think of myself as Metacomet, son of Massasoit, and sachem of the Wampanoags.

"Tobias, my counselor, how I need your wise words now to help guide me through the complications your death has brought," I said softly to the air.

My reverie was broken by the arrival into the wigwam of Wootonekanuske. The beautiful one. My wife.

"There is much unhappiness among the tribe. The younger ones especially are hot for English blood."

"It is not time," I said. "Not yet. We are not ready."

"But Tobias's blood must be avenged, my husband. The English must be taught that Indian blood is as good as English blood, that our people are as important as their own."

"And they will be. In good time."

"When will that time be? Philip. . ." she caught herself, "Metacomet, you have been striving for years to ready us, to prepare us for what must come. When will it be time? Are you so sure the time is not now?"

I sat silently. My wife spoke my own inner arguments, my own questions, questions for which I had no answer. Only days before I had ended a weeks long celebration and dance held to entice younger warriors from other tribes to join me, to pressure their own sachems to join me. They had come from every tribe, from the Nipmucks to the North and the Narragansetts to the West. They had come from what remained of the once-proud Pequods, and from the Niantics. I know as well as any that tribe leadership depends as much on consensus as it does on an individual sachem's power. And leadership outside of one's immediate tribe rests solely on the agreement of those being led.

But now I was caught in the middle of the situation I had worked so long and hard to create. Young warriors were hot for English blood. They wanted to attack now. I could lead them into battle tomorrow and they would follow me to their deaths.

But the older leaders, such as Awashonks of the Sakkonets, still feared the strength of the English. They feared that, even with my long years of preparation, when it came to war other tribes of the Algonquin would not join together with us to fight the English. It was the old attitude, brought on in large part by my own father, Massasoit, legendary friend of the Pilgrims.

My father had nursed the English through their first harsh winters when, left to their own, they would have surely perished from their ignorance. And my father had preached peace and cooperation with the English, even after their massacre of the Pequod seventeen years after their arrival. He'd held to this course right up to the time of his death a decade ago.

And now the old leaders who had followed him were blind to the danger I so clearly saw. The way of the white man was to overwhelm. The English numbers would soon be too great, their needs too large to be contained. I had come to see they could not contain themselves. For even those among them who sincerely wanted peace with us could not stop the settlement of the ancient lands, the plowing under of the hunting grounds which had been kept free of forest for years. They could not be controlled even by their own leaders.

They had to be stopped.

But the old ones among us must now be made to see this, and it was the young who must make them. Their pressure, their insistence, must continue until even the old ones could not resist. Then all the tribes of the Algonquians would rise as one, and push the white men back into the sea. This is my vision.

But only if we came together. And though I knew the time was rapidly coming when we'd have to choose between our ways and the English way, I wasn't sure all the possible contacts had been completed, all the arguments in tribal councils had been made, to sustain war now.

Or was I underestimating my own years of work?

"I must go," I said, rising from his blanket. "I will seek out the advice of the powaw. Perhaps his wisdom can help me see the way."

"Do that, my husband," my wife said, putting her hand comfortingly upon my shoulder. "I tell you only what is being said. But it is yours to decide. And I take comfort in knowing that."

I took her hand and squeezed it. With a resigned smile, I left in search of the powaw.

I found the old man bent over a fire, boiling sweet smelling herbs in a clay pot. The old man looked up as my shadow fell upon him.

"Ahhh, Metacomet, I am glad you have come. Please sit." He motioned to a log drawn near the fire. I sat. "Inhale deeply, the scent will relax you."

I did as instructed, and indeed, the strong aroma of the brew did take away the tightness from my arms and neck. I closed my eyes and inhaled again, letting the fumes overcome me.

"So, what brings our sachem to this old man?" the powaw asked, settling his thin frame next to mine on the log.

I opened my eyes, suddenly aware once more of the fire, and the steam rising from the pot.

"It is the same matter as before, only now more urgent. Tobias's death under the English law has enraged the younger ones. They are unruly. I'm not certain I can control them. I'm also not certain if I should."

"Do you fear the English will come for you next?"

"I'm sure I will be sent for. You cannot murder the counselor without also wishing to kill the one he counseled." I turned to the powaw. "I need to know if you have any knowledge, any visions of what the future holds?"

"Visions? You have never been one for my visions. In my advice, you have found wisdom, and for that I give thanks to nature. But you have not asked for visions before."

"I ask now."

The old man turned to the fire, closed his eyes and inhaled, holding his breath for several moments before slowly releasing it.

"I have had dreams," he said, without opening his eyes. "I have had dreams of war between the white man and the red." His eyes tightened as he went on. "I have seen much misery and bloodshed, much pain and sorrow. But," he said, and now his eyes opened, "I have also seen joy in victory – successes against the enemy – all are mixed together."

"That does not help me," I said, now with a touch of impatience. "War always brings both joy and sorrow. I need to know if now is the time to attack. If now is the time to go forward. Can you tell me that?"

The powaw again turned to me and stared into my black eyes. "I can tell you only this. I have dreamed that a warrior first kills an Englishman, and that brings on the war in which, in the end, the English prevail."

"But what if the English strike first? What outcome then?"

The powaw shrugged. "I do not know. There is no vision there. No dream. But know this, if the Algonquin kills first, we are lost."

I considered this. "You are right, my old friend, I do not put much faith in your dreams. But others do, including the young warriors." I paused, thinking. "What I need now is more time. Every day will be a help. Do this for me. Let your vision be known. Let the warriors know the spirits tell you we cannot draw first blood in battle. Then they will wait."

"Wait for what, Metacomet?" said the old man, staring into the fire.

I was saved from answering by a young boy, running into the clearing from the well worn path.

"Metacomet! You are needed in the village," gasped the boy, panting from his exertion. "It is the English. They have come for you. They say they wish to talk with you."

I rose to go with the boy, but turned at the forest's edge. "Do as I say, powaw. Tell them."

The powaw stared at me from his fire, inhaling deeply the relaxing scents. "Last night's dream - so much pain and sorrow. So little joy, on either side. For once I felt glad to be old, glad to not have to face what you and the others now have to." He inhaled deeply from the bowl.

I went into the trees and brush,the boy only a few steps behind.

"It is our hope that the troubles between your race and ours can still be settled, that we can return to that happy state that we existed in just a few years ago," John Easton, deputy Governor of Rhode Island, was saying to the warriors gathered with me in front of him. I sat in their midst. "Not all of us are as excitable as the Plymouth colony men. Cooler heads can prevail. But only if they are given the chance. We are asking you for that chance." He looked directly at me.

"Peace is always preferable to war," I replied non-commitally.

Easton shifted uneasily on his feet. He'd been dealing with our tribes for some time now, and there had always been a comfort between us. The Rhode Islanders and our people have always been friendly. Often Rhode Island played peacemaker when troubles between us and the other English colonies flared up, and I knew they hoped to do so now. But never before had I felt, or Easton faced, the resentment which now burned in the eyes of the warriors surrounding me.

"Please then, there must be a path to peace," he pleaded. "Tell us where it is so that we might convince others to follow it. We have told you Plymouth plans no further actions against you on the Sassamon murder. It is over."

"It ended three lives too late," I said, and grunts of approval were offered up by the warriors.

"It couldn't be otherwise. One of your own people testified he saw the murder. . ."

"One of our own?" I roared. "In skin, perhaps, but not in spirit. The Indian that testified is little more than a snake. He was in heavy debt to Tobias, and in his testimony he saw an easy way to end the debt. Why wasn't that brought out at your English trial?"

Easton shifted uneasily on his feet. "Whatever his reasons, the fact is he still testified against them. It is not the fault of the Plymouth jury that he did so."

"Tell me," I said, my voice rising to drown out both the deputy Governor's voice and the general murmur from both Indians and whites. "Why is it that your English juries are so ready to believe an Indian who speaks against another Indian, but if an Indian speaks against an Englishman, it is as if the Indian has no tongue?"

There were hoots and hollers from behind me. I was clearly speaking their thoughts, and admit to purposely whipping up their fury. I could hear the little optimism Easton still held seep from him, replaced by a cold desperation.

"I agree, great sachem, that your people have not always been treated justly, especially by the Plymouthers. But still war is in the air, a war that will benefit no one, least of all the Indian. Can't you see? It will only be used as an excuse

by those English who wish your destruction to send you all to your deaths. Look instead at the history of peace between our peoples. . ."

"The history!?" I thundered, and as I did so I felt a power surge through me, a power of the warriors of old, of a long a noble history the made up hundreds of years of Algonquin pride. "I will tell you of the history. The English who first came to this country were but a handful of people, poor and distressed. My father, Massasoit, was sachem. He relieved their distress, and treated them with kindness and hospitality. He gave them land to build and plant on. He did all he could to serve them. They became friends.

"But soon more English came, and then still more. They brought with them guns, which the Indian did not have. And they brought their law, and used those guns to impose their law on the Indian.

"My father's counselors grew worried, and bid my father to attack the Englishmen before they became too strong, to push them back into the sea from which they had come. But my father resisted, remembering his early friendships, and argued there was much to learn from the English in the way of growing crops and raising of cattle and fruits. He said there was more than enough land for both the English and the Indian to prosper.

"His advice prevailed, and further aid was given to the English.

"But experience has shown my father wrong and his counselors' right. The English continued to gain our land. They took our fishing grounds and our hunting grounds as their own. And yet my father remained a friend to them until he died.

"My older brother, whom you called Alexander, became sachem. When he resisted meeting the demands for more land, the English pretended to suspect him of evil designs against them. He was seized, confined, and thrown into sickness from which he died. Soon after I become sachem, they tried to disarm all of my people. They hauled my people into their courts tried my people under their laws and by their customs, and put fines upon us which we could not pay, then took our lands in 'payment'."

The Englishman grew silent, but the warriors voiced their agreement with my history. I looked about. There was no turning back now. My speech had not only convinced those around me, it had committed me to the course I had so longed planned and argued for, but had only now stepped upon. My decision was made, the path chosen. I signaled for silence, and when the murmurs had stopped, I plunged on.

"A line was drawn between our people, one which, in the interest of peace, I agreed to with the English. But when English cattle wandered upon our lands and become lost, I would be seized until I sold yet another tract of my country for cattle we had 'taken.' Thus tract after tract is gone. Only a small part of my

ancestors' land now remains." I stood taller and turned my gaze slowly about the room, demanding in my sudden silence the full attention of all before I finished.

"I am determined not to live until I have no country."

I turned and stalked through the crowd of Indians, now standing, hollering, and shaking their fists in happy agreement with so just a cause. As I disappeared down the village street to the path leading back to my own land, the Indian multitude followed me, leaving only the small delegation of Rhode Islanders behind.

Later I heard that when we were lost to sight, Easton turned with a heavy heart to the dozen men still gathered with him and said, "May God have mercy on our souls, for I believe that before the next full moon, blood will run thick upon our lands." He was an insightful man.

Meanwhile the powaw's cautionary vision had the effect I hoped for. While warriors looted and killed cattle, no Algonquin dared tempt the spirits by killing an Englishman.

I valued the time gained. I sent off delegations made up of my most trusted warriors to seek out Matoonas of the Nipmucks, Awashonks of the Sakkonets, and Canonchet of the Narragansetts, tribal leaders whom I sensed were sympathetic towards my ideas. I went myself went to see Weetamoo, squaw sachem of the Pocassets, a tribe long supportive of the Wampanoags.

"It is finally time," I stated to her. "We must rise against the white men and drive them from our lands."

"How can we? You yourself have told me that we cannot defeat them without the allegiance of the Narragansetts and Nipmucks. Do you now have those allegiances?"

"No," I admitted with a despair I could not hide from her. "But I now feel they will not come until it has begun. War will force them to choose, force them to see where their interest lies. Their people are already with us. I have told you of the dances and feasts I have held. Hundreds of warriors came. They will come again to my side in war, even if their leaders do not. Then their leaders must follow."

"So why do you come to me now?"

"You more than any should understand. You know the English. They killed my brother, your husband. They have taken your lands, and tried your people under their laws."

"But they are strong," she argued. "My friend, Church, came and told me this. He would not lie. They have many guns. They have soldiers."

"If they are so strong, they would not now be pleading with you to stay out. Their soldiers are no match for our warriors. And we have guns also."

"Not in the numbers of the English."

"We have enough. We will never have more than they. As each season passes they grow stronger, and we grow weaker. Can't you see? More and more of them come with every ship. They bring more weapons, more tools, and the need for even more land. They bring disease. Our people number less than half what they once did because of their disease. And when they need more land they will bring another."

I looked carefully at Weetamoo. She had aged much since her wedding day to my older brother. She had been lovely then, a young, slim, carefree girl with a smile that flickered onto her face easily, and never more easily than on the day of their marriage. It had, of course, been many years since that day. Alexander had been dead thirteen winters. But it was more than time. It was the strain of leading her people in these troubled times. Times of submission to the English. Times when the ancient strength and dignity of her people had been eroded. I knew her well, and knew her answer before she spoke it.

"I will join with you, if only to honor the memory of my husband, your brother. One does not easily forget treachery."

I settled back in the bearskin robe I sat on. "Good. I am glad. We have little time. Call in your best warriors. We must plan what we can with the time that remains."

Swansea – June 24, 1675

Thomas Kendall sat with old Josiah Hawkins, glancing every now and then across the fields they guard while the rest of the town attended a special fast and prayer service at the church.

"Quite lucky, if you ask me, getting guard duty the way we did," Hawkins said, his feet resting on an old chopping stump he'd had the boy bring over, along with a chair from inside the house. "The preacher is a little long-winded for my tastes."

Thomas looked at the old man with surprise. He'd often thought the same thing, but he hadn't realized adults might too. His parents had brought him up to believe the preacher was pretty much perfect. Thomas believed it was his own fault he found the minister's sermons dull, even on a hot summer day.

"Damn Indians," Hawkins went on, the profanity shocking Thomas even more. His mother and father never swore, and would have beat him hard if he had. He knew that for a fact, because his brother had sworn once. Only once.

"Why are the Indians causing so much trouble?" Thomas asked.

"Cause they're lazy good for nothings," Hawkins said, then spit for emphasis. "That's why. They're used to having everything handed to them. Women do all the work in them Indian towns, you know. All the men do is hunt and fish and play with them infernal dogs all day. They ain't never done a hard day's work. None of them. Then they sell you land, and the next thing you know they're back on it again, hunting and fishing and stripping off the berries like they'd never sold it to you in the first place."

Thomas shook his head in wonder. He was learning a lot this Thursday afternoon. More, he was sure, than if he was with everyone else in church. Thomas had known there was Indian trouble. Everyone knew that. Indians had been looting empty houses and stealing cattle for days. Everyone talked about how people had seen Indians all painted up for war, marching to join up with Philip, the Indian name everyone repeated with a fearful look.

"What do you know about Philip?" Thomas asked. As long as he was learning so much, he'd try to learn more.

"You mean 'King Philip'" the man said sarcastically.

"Is he a King?"

"Seems to think he is. He's been brewing up trouble for years. Most Indians are peaceable enough left alone. But old King Philip, he talks at them and talks at them, and gets them all riled up with lies about what white men did here or there. I tell you, young man, if we Englishmen were half the devils old King Phil makes us out to be, we'd have strung him up years ago. Probably should have."

"Why haven't we?"

"Laws, son. We got laws. Can't go stringing people up without proof of no crime. It's what separates us from them savages. And Philip, he's a wily one. I'll say that for him. Can't never prove nothing against him. Say, what's that?"

The old man pointed across the field to where a few cows were grazing contentedly in the sun. Thomas didn't see anything.

"Go get the gun from the house," Hawkins instructed. Thomas still didn't see anything, but he did as he was told, fetching the heavy flintlock, already primed and ready to shoot, and offering it to Hawkins.

"No boy. You hold on to it, and do as I say. These old hands aren't as steady as they once was." He peered across the field. "There, see him now?"

Thomas did see him now. An Indian had crept in among the cows, approaching one very slowly, a shiny object which could only be a knife held downward in his raised hand.

"Draw a bead on him." Thomas still stared, and Hawkins had to repeat the instruction before he raised the flintlock to his shoulder. "You a good shot son?"

"I've hit my share of squirrels," Thomas boasted.

"Good. Well, draw in tight. Get him in your sight."

Thomas did so, just as the Indian plunged the knife into the neck of the unsuspecting cow, which let out a low moan quickly stopped by the knife being drawn across its throat.

"Shoot! Shoot now, dammit," Hawkins yelled, rising out of his chair.

Thomas squeezed the trigger and felt the hard jerk of the gunstock against his shoulder. Through the gun's smoke he saw the Indian stand up straight, let out a small cry, then slump into the grass out of sight.

"Good shot, young fellow. A good piece of work."

"Shouldn't we go get him?" Thomas asked, staring awestruck across the field.

"No. Where there's one Indian, there's bound to be more. We head out into that field and there's no telling how many of them might fall on us. Best to stay here. And reload that gun."

Thomas didn't have to be told that twice.

"Oh merciful God," the preacher shouted in prayer from the front of the small church, "Look down upon us sinners and have mercy upon us. Calm the vengeful heart of the savage and restore peace to our land. But if thou shall not, then give us strength and courage to meet the foe and destroy him, and in so doing spread your word. Amen." The congregation echoed him.

"I think it best if we all go back to the garrison houses, instead of lingering here after the service," the minister said before leaving the front of the church.

The worshippers obediently rose and went to the rear, the men taking up their guns as they did so.

Three men, led by the reliable John Billingsley, went to check the fields where the main body of cattle grazed. They walked past a clearing, through a small wood, then into the pasture, keeping their guns poised for action. In these tense times one couldn't be too careful. But all they saw was a dozen cows grazing peacefully in the distance.

"All quiet here. Let's go back to the others," Billingsley said, hoisting his gun over his shoulders and draping his wrists over either end. The other two kept their rifles ready, watching behind them as they headed back to the forest, in case trouble lay at their rear.

But the crack of the first volley came from the forest in front of them. Billingsley went down in a heap, a ball through his neck. The other two turned, raised their guns quickly to their shoulder, and fired wildly at the puffs of smoke rising from the trees. As they did a blood curdling scream came from behind them.

They turned again to see a half-dozen Indian warriors, some with guns, some with tomahawks, bearing down on them.

"Christ Jesus," one muttered, then pulled a knife from his belt before feeling the ripping, stinging thud of a ball in his thigh. He went down screaming.

The other man stared at his two fallen friends, one yelling in pain, the other silent in death, then at the Indians now only a few yards away. Instinctively he threw his arms up over his head in cover, and felt the slicing of a tomahawk driving through his arms. He fell, mercifully senseless, to the ground.

A warrior came up to the one wounded in the thigh, pulled a knife from his belt, grabbed the man's hair and pulled back hard, exposing his neck to the knife he held aloft.

"Dear God! Dear god save me!" the man screamed, then closed his eyes is preparation for the blow.

It never came. Instead he heard the welcome yells of Englishmen and the whiz of musket balls thudding into the earth near him. The Indian dropped hold of his hair and ran with the others across the fields and into the woods. He sank back on the ground, gulping in huge swallows of air. "Thank you, Lord. Praise and thank you." He reached down to his thigh and felt the warm, sticky ooze of his blood cover his hand. He gasped again, then passed out.

The Kendalls arrived back from church to collect their son and old Mr. Hawkins and head to the garrison house.

"I shot one! I shot an Indian!" Thomas boasted with a boisterous pride he did not fully feel inside.

Thomas's father looked at Hawkins, who nodded confirmation.

"Bastard was stealing your cows. Tommy here got him fair and square."

Thomas's parents exchanged worried glances, then Mr. Kendall ordered everyone to gather what they could together in the few moments he felt they safely had. While they did, he went to the window. He stared hard, then looked to Hawkins.

"I think the Indians might be wanting revenge," he said to Hawkins in a manner that conveyed blame as well as concern. "I see a few gathering out on the edge of the field, and they look to be coming this way."

"Well, gather us all up. They'll never attack a party as big as we are," Hawkins stated.

Mr. Kendall was doubtful, but there was nothing else to be done now. He gathered the muskets, made certain they were all primed and ready, and gave one each to Hawkins and Thomas.

"Let's get to the garrison house," he said to his family. They set out cautiously, Kendall leading. Thomas and Hawkins bringing up the rear.

They were fifty yards away from their home when the first arrows fell among them.

"If they are to live, we must get a surgeon," Joshua Browne said to no one particular.

"That will mean going to Plymouth," his wife, Abigail, said. "Forty miles."

"Still we must, if they are to have a chance. One death today is enough."

"I'm afraid it isn't," said George Leach as he came through the garrison's door and swung his own musket down to his side.

"What do you mean?" Abigail asked, afraid to hear the answer.

"Just came back from the Kendall place. All dead. All six of them."

"Even Tom?" Abigail refused to believe war could so quickly claim a boy.

"Afraid so, Ma'am. Those savages weren't too particular about age. Or sex."

Joshua Browne looked around the garrison house. "Is everyone else in? Where are the Leveretts?"

"I saw them go into the other fort house," a voice in the corner called out. "I suspect everyone else is in one now, too. Everyone with any sense, and if there's one thing Indian trouble does, it brings common sense to people, real quick."

"That it does, Edward," agreed Joshua Browne grimly. He looked around. "I need someone to go with me to Plymouth to fetch the surgeon." There was a deep silence, broken after a moment by his wife.

"Joshua, you can't."

"I have to. I can't stand by and watch good men die. We'll go after dark. The Indians will have gone off by then." He gazed around the room. "How about it?"

Edward stepped forward. "I'll go with you, Joshua."

"Just a minute ago you talked of common sense coming to people," Abigail said crossly. "Now you've taken leave of your own." Edward stared silently down at his boots at this tongue lashing.

"Now Abby, we'll be fine," Joshua soothed her. From the floor above them a pained cry pierced the air as one of the wounded men gasped desperately for breath. "And they'll be dead if we don't get help back soon. It's settled. We'll go after dark."

As dusk settled, the families huddled in the garrison house looked sadly out at the glowing embers of what had been, at the start of the day, sturdy homes and barns full with the first cutting of hay. Throughout the day they'd watched silently as Indian parties methodically burned and wrecked anything out of shooting distance of the two fortified garrison houses. Men and wives clung to each other and wept as the work of two, four or eight years went up in a smoky cloud. As the burning continued, the silent, fearful realization came to them all. This was no simple, if terrifying, Indian raid. This was war.

When darkness came Joshua Browne picked up his rifle, touched Edward's arm, and headed to the door. Abigail grabbed Joshua to her and clung, weeping.

"You'd better come back to me, Joshua Browne. Come back safe, or you'll have the devil to pay."

Joshua Browne returned the hold, then stepped back from it. "I will. I promise." He smiled a false smile of encouragement, and Abigail smiled back weakly. "Take care now," he said, and with a soft kiss on her forehead, stepped to the door.

"Dowse the lights," he commanded, and the candles and lamps in the room were covered or put out. Only with the darkness as complete inside as out did he carefully swing the door open and, followed by Edward, slip into the night.

"Come back, Joshua Browne," Abigail whispered quietly again.

Under the bright sun of the following day, two men, one burly, one thin, traveled quickly along the well worn path from Plymouth to Swansea, sent from Boston on a mission of peace to King Philip. There were reports of tension along the frontier, and Massachusetts Bay leaders did not trust their fellow leaders in Plymouth Bay to handle events with tact. If war could be avoided, they would be the ones to foster this.

"Not much further now. I recognize the bend ahead. Another mile and we'll be to Swansea," the burlier one said. They walked to the bend, then around it.

"Lord protect us," the thin one said, eyes fixed firmly on the scene in front of him, thinking only to pull his gun closer and pull back the hammer. They remained motionless for a few moments before the burly one spoke.

"I deem it expedient to declare this peace mission at an end. Let us go back the way we came and report on this. . . most unfortunate passing." The two men turned and trotted back along the path, scrutinizing the forest all around them for any sign of Indians, and leaving behind them the bloody, mutilated remains of Joshua Browne and Edward.

"While we waste our energies in plunder and looting, the English army approaches. We must be prepared to meet them," I argued as the flame from the fire flickered light upon my face. "And we cannot meet them as we are now."

"Why not?" asked one of the young braves, who called himself Charles in the English fashion. "Have we not already shown our courage? Our determination? Have we not already won great victories against the English?"

"We have," I replied, "Of our bravery there is no doubt. Tremendous victories have been ours." I didn't want to dampen the joy of these younger braves. But neither could I afford to let them run wild. "But the army comes, and while we will certainly be victorious if we use our cunning and skills, victory will only be assured with planning and preparation."

"What would you have us do?" Charles asked with excitement.

"Pull back across the water. Use our victories over the English to draw still more warriors to our fight. Then join with the Nipmucks and Narragansetts to overcome all the English invaders."

"The Narragansetts are our enemies as much as the English," Charles spat out, then moderated his tone. While his bravery of the last few days had earned him the right to be heard in council, it did not give him the right to be disrespectful to me. "Why should not victory over the English be ours alone? Why seek peace with one enemy to defeat another in battle?"

"It is not battle," I insisted. "These Englishmen are not like the Narragansetts, or even like the Mohawks with all their fierceness and pride. Winning a single battle against them means nothing. Only battle after battle after battle will convince them they should not continue to make a home here."

"But already their people have fled before us."

"Until their army comes. Then they will be back, and more will follow them. It is their way." I looked at the older, wise men of the tribe, joined now by several younger members new to the council fires, but necessary to the decisions that would be made in the coming days. The young men were hot with the fire of battle, the taste of blood already in their mouths, young men who could not yet imagine their own deaths despite having already caused the deaths of others. Young men like Charles.

"To retreat now, to go to the Nipmucks for help, will only be seen by the English as a sign of weakness." Charles argued. "It will embolden them to come after us still further."

"And when they do," I replied with steady determination, "When they come after us, all of us, when they come after the whole Algonquin nation, then they will be crushed." I wasn't certain of this, but I had to make them believe it if they were to have even a chance in a war on the English.

"Metacomet speaks wisely," said a young warrior, older than Charles, but still young. "Let the Englishmen have their day, if they wish it so. Let them believe that in our victories they see their own. It will only make our final victory that much sweeter."

I felt satisfaction. The young warrior's support meant my arguments had reached those they had to reach. Some of the hot headed ones would still be discontented, but most were with me now. And they all would follow.

"I still say we should fight them here," Charles said, but I noticed he had lost his strident tone. Humiliation was not necessary.

"Your words are the words of a brave young warrior, Charles. They deserve the consideration they have received, because of your noble feats in battle. Believe that they have not fallen on deaf ears. But now is not the time. Be certain, however, that the time for your words is not far off."

Charles, soothed by my words, sat down upon his deerskin quietly, ready to do as he was instructed. I smiled proudly on him.

"We have no time to waste," I said, asserting my reconfirmed command. "My scouts have told me the English approach with many men, and many guns. If they attack us here, with our back to the water on three sides, we shall never have the chance to join with our Nipmuck brothers. Let us make ready to move the village to the western bank."

As the council broke up I lingered by the fire, listening as my orders were now relayed to the rest of the tribe. Within a day, two at the most, we would be ready to move.

It took longer than I planned. If it had been an army of warriors we would have been on the paths north within hours. But there were children, and animals, and the old ones to be moved. Many of the older women could not understand moving in the middle of the growing season, and from where fish were also plentiful in the sea surrounding us.

I set warriors to work collecting canoes and rafts of all sorts. If we could not move overland off the peninsula before the English blocked its entrance, I wanted to be ready to get away over the water. The wisdom of this was confirmed by a report brought from the young warrior Charles, who I had sent to scout the whereabouts of the English army.

"The main body approaches the neck," Charles excitedly reported. "We cannot leave over land. The chance has passed us."

I told the warrior next to him to spread the word among the village to begin loading the canoes. When he was gone, I turned my attention back to Charles, who was still obviously excited.

"You have more to tell me."

"As I said, the main body is rapidly approaching. But as we circled back to the village, we came upon an advance party of eight men."

"Are they soon here?" I asked with concern.

"They are dead," Charles reported with a glow of satisfaction. My hand began to knead the inside of my thighs as I sat, cross-legged, before the small fire on which fish were being dried out for the journey ahead. Charles grew concerned that he had somehow displeased me, but he needn't have worried.

"We need to delay the Englishmen. We need to strike fear into their hearts, to stall them. If only for a day."

"I will lead an attack against them," Charles volunteered, "A small attack, to make them halt for a few moments."

"A good plan. Very good. You are learning to think ahead, Charles." Charles smiled at my praise. "But I need all the warriors here to continue the move. Also, it would be a waste of lives, lives we can't afford to lose."

Charles looked confused. "How then do we delay them?"

"The English scare easily, if the right scare is applied. Gather two other braves and return to where you killed the advance party. Cut off their heads and put them on poles in the path of the advancing army."

"As the English did to Tobias."

"Yes. Coming upon them in the forest will cause them to hesitate, and give us the time we need to escape the trap we have created for ourselves. Go now, and return quickly. We leave the camp by night."

Charles left. Wootonekanuske came from their wigwam and sat by me.

"Where do we go from here, my husband?"

"We will stay on the other shore until the English come close to chase us out. Then we will head north, to the Nipmucks. Matoonas has already given his pledge to join with us against the English. Muttawmp also. Once together, we will be able to turn on this army the English has sent. Without their strength, we can come to no good here."

"It is hard to leave the ancient lands." she said sadly, but without rancor.

"It is," I agreed, slapping my thigh to signal Three Toes to come lie at my side. "I have always taken strength from the land, from Monthaup. My heart breaks at leaving. But I leave so that when I return, I will do so knowing it will never be taken from us. Never."

As I now stared into the fire, I could feel Wootonekanuske look proudly upon me, her husband, Metacomet - sachem of the Wampanoags.

"They are celebrating as if they have won a great victory," Charles reported to me. I stared off at the flickering campfires of the English upon the hill of Monthaup. The thought of them occupying my homeland rankled me, but I controlled my anger in front of Charles.

"If they believe victory lies in taking empty land, let them have their celebration. Imagine their despair when it is taken from them."

"Still, it angers me to see them so."

"It angers me also," I allowed.

"Then why do we not attack?"

"The river. Whoever crosses it first has it at their back. A river at your back limits you. It gives you no room to retreat, should it be necessary. If we attack, it would be with the river at our back. If they attack, it will be at theirs. We will wait for their attack."

"Why wait to drive them back across the river, to our homeland? Why not go to Matoonas and return in strength?"

I smiled for the first time in many days. "Because once they cross the river, and we drive them back into it, the English will no longer celebrate their victories. Instead they will weep. That is how I want to leave them."

The boats drew up on the shore, and the men waded through the dark, cold water at the wide river's bank, wetting their boots and making them uncomfortable as they stepped onto land. The boats then pulled a safe distance off the bank to avoid ambush while the men were away. There were two dozen in all, armed with cutlasses and with new flintlocks, those marvels of design. Only a decade before, the matchlock had been the standard gun. Heavy and cumbersome, the matchlock had to be carried, set up on a tripod, aimed as best it could before a fire, lit from another source and touched to the hole, set off the powder. In the heat of battle, with arrows flying all around, this time spent reloading could be deadly.

But flintlocks were self-contained. When loaded and primed, a pull of the trigger sent the hammer, a piece of flint firmly wedged between its two metal grips, forward into the firing pan, the flint striking the metal and creating a spark, setting off the powder through a small hole in the barrel.

Slimmer, easier to aim than the matchlocks, in trained hands the guns could fire three shots a minute, cutting through any attacking group with deadly accuracy at short range.

Left only in the hands of the English, the flintlock could have been the turning point in the war against the Indians, another Agincourt, where the small, tired English army had destroyed the magnificent French armies armed with the new, deadly range and accuracy of the longbow.

But the Indians also had the flintlock, and it had been provided by the English themselves - in efforts to establish goodwill in some cases, in order to make quick profits in most others. Selling guns to the Indians was a frowned upon but much practiced profession. The result was that the Indian hordes now facing this small band of Englishmen who had crossed the bay waters to the Pocasset Swamp were armed with guns as fine and accurate as their own.

Which was why, as they took their first tentative steps onto the grassy bank and then forward into the bushy areas beyond, they carefully searched the area around them, sensitive to sudden movements or sounds. Their commander, Benjamin Church, formed them into a tight squad and moved them forward quickly. It was his view that this war could best be ended now, with quick and decisive action.

Most of the men with Church agreed instead with the other commanders still at King Phillip's captured camp. They felt they had already won a great victory in driving the Indians from the peninsula. Chasing down Phillip now was unnecessary. Let him come crawling back when his food ran short.

But, under Church's urgings, the commanders had authorized this small excursion. Church himself thought it too small for the job, but accepted command hoping he could prove his point. The Indians could be beaten, he believed, but they weren't beaten yet.

The small troop crossed down into Punkatees Neck, then stopped short at the sight of an Indian wigwam. A few men were dispatched to scout it. They crept carefully up to it, then one peeked in and grinned.

"Ain't nothing in here but a whole bunch of skins and foods." Hearing him, several others rushed forward, intent on getting themselves some of the valuable pelts.

"Stop it," Church bellowed. "Come out of that infernal wigwam and form up. Don't forget you're soldiers, at least for now. And I dare say you'll have your hands full enough in a little while without having them full of plunder. Get away from there now."

Grumbling, the men did as ordered. They were not used to military life. Most had been at it less than a week, and several thought it was a week too long.

They reached a place Church recognized as a pea field that belonged to Captain Almy, one of the first whites to settle this bank of the river. Abandoned when trouble began, signs of even this few weeks of forced neglect showed the crop already overtaken by the weeds which grew so fast in this rich, damp soil.

Church divided his command into two companies as they crossed the field, taking personal command of one.

Suddenly he spied two Indians, flintlocks at their side, walking towards them across the field. He signaled his men to fall flat, out of sight, and they did, but the other group remained standing. The Indians saw them, turned and ran.

"Come back, you rascals," Church yelled. "I want to talk with you. No harm will come." But the Indians continued to run, and one, climbing up over a fence at the edge of a field, turned and fired at the troops behind him.

The bullet whined over their heads and a man lying beside Church sprung up and fired a return shot. The Indian who had fired spun around the top of the fence and screamed, but still managed to crawl into the thickets, where he was lost from view.

Encouraged, the rest of the troops rose and bounded forward after the game. The hunt was on, and the fox was wounded.

As I watched the English troops hurry through the brushy field, I turned to the warriors I had positioned so carefully when word first came that the English were crossing the bay. I waited as the Englishmen came closer and closer, until it seemed the Englishmen were nearly on top of us, then I waved a long stick.

Instantly a volley of sixty shots tore across the field and into the incoming Englishmen, halting them in their tracks. Those not cut down stood confused, peering into the smoke that had suddenly risen up from the field in front of them. One man raised his gun to his shoulder and fired into the haze. Others followed, firing at an enemy they could not see.

I fingered my hatchet, ready to spring forward and lead the attack when the English had spent their shots. I had let them approach to where they had no chance of reloading their weapons before my warriors fell upon them. But then, above the crack of the gunfire, I heard the voice of the English commander.

"Hold your fire, damn you, or the lot of them will be down on us so fast all our heads will be hanging from sticks." The firing stopped, and the English began to retreat in order.

I stood and signaled my men to try surrounding the English. I would cut them off from the riverbank and from any hope of escape in the boats waiting off the bank.

But their leader also saw the danger. "Run men," he yelled as they drew out of range of where our first volley had come. "Run for that wall yonder, and form up there. Beat 'em to it lads, or say goodbye to life."

The men did as he directed without further urging, scampering to the promised safety of the stone wall standing near the edge of the field within sight of the shore.

With their head start, the Englishmen easily outran us to the wall, reformed in good order, and started to return gunfire at us as they signaled wildly for the boats to come get them. My attempt to destroy the small squad had failed. I quickly surveyed how to make the best use of the chances still available to us.

"Charles, take some warriors to the high ground - there," I said, motioning to a small rise well to the north of the English band.

"Our guns will have no accuracy from that distance," protested Charles.

"Those of us here will have the necessary accuracy, but we will also have a stone wall to shoot through. From there, you will be able to shoot behind it. It may take many shots to reach them, but they will be there for some time. I have sent warriors to the shore to shoot at any boats which try to land. We may not take their lives from them, but at least we will show them that the Wampanoag is not to be trifled with."

Charles nodded in enlightened agreement and trotted off to carry out his mission.

I spent the rest of the long afternoon urging on my warriors, making sure the fire upon the Englishmen never let up, making certain that powder and balls were brought up timely to those who fired so the rain of lead would not slacken.

We made the English farmers turned soldiers regret the day they had joined this army. I had turned what had started out as high adventure for them into a battle for their lives.

But the English commander, Church, made good use of what little cover the ground afforded him. Now I was sorry that a larger force had not come over. Two dozen men could hide from the onslaught of fire I had ordered. A hundred could not have. But still I took grim satisfaction as the afternoon wore on. I had proven to my warriors we could drive off the English, proven that, under my leadership, we could claim victories. I had proven it to my warriors, and more importantly, I had proven it to myself.

Sharp fighting continued during the next few days between the English and us. Their leader, Church, had managed to get his tiny command off the riverbank that first day as night fell and darkness covered his retreat. But the English had not given up. Instead they came back across the water with still larger parties. I noted they now crossed more carefully.

My warriors held them off with fierce ambushes and well executed attacks, but it was becoming plain that the English were not going to turn tail and run. They built a fortress on my homeland at Monthaup, to use as a base for continued operations. I realized the time had come to leave and join with the Nipmucks to the north.

But meanwhile I used the delay afforded by fighting the English to further push my arguments with the Nipmuck leaders. I sent parties of my most skillful speakers to tell of our resistance. I regretted only that I could not go myself, for above all I was confident of my abilities to persuade. But my presence here, in the face of the enemy, was too important.

"You are working too hard," Wootonekanuske scolded me as she dished out some squirrel stew she heated on the fire in the center of the temporary wigwam. I had laid down on a robe, closing my eyes and trying to rest despite the heat of the mid-July day. "You do not have to do everything. Lead your warriors. Leave others to oversee the move of the village. Perhaps it is not done as quickly. It is still done."

"But it must be done quickly. The English continue to bring more troops to their fort. It becomes harder and harder to turn them back."

"Surely the new warriors help. More come every day." Wootonekanuske's growing pride was evident with each warrior that joined our fight. Dozens came to the camp every day, from tribes as near as the Narragansetts, and as far as the Mohegans, drawn by the resistance to English rule "King Philip" - as I was still called by others - now symbolized.

"They are heartening. But to defeat the English we need whole tribes, not just young hotheads."

"They are more than hotheads, my husband. They are the flower of their tribes," Wootonekanuske reproached me.

I smiled. "I don't insult the young ones. They are exactly what we need to carry out what we have begun. But until we have the great tribes with us we cannot even try for the victories we must have to defeat the English."

I sat up, took the bowl of stew from her and spooned out a meaty mouthful. The stew's heat added to the heat of the day, but I had not eaten since the night before, and it felt good in my stomach. As I ate Wootonekanuske talked about our nine year old son, and the skill he had shown in hunting the squirrels from which she'd made the stew.

"Two arrows, two squirrels. Both clean shots, right through the midsections. He already has the warrior's eye."

"The test will come when he learns the gun. The bow is outdated. In a few years it will be of no matter in battle. Even now its value is limited to the surprise it affords before the noise of the guns make all else fall into the background."

"You should teach him to shoot then."

"I want to. I want to spend time teaching him all he will need to know. And I will. But not now. Afterwards. After this is over. Now I must return to my work. I have wasted enough time."

"I remember when time spent with me was not considered such a waste," Wootonekanuske said with a sly smile.

"Time spent with you is never a waste, my wife. Once again you make me see the truth where I could only see the problems." I lingered a moment, letting my hand fall lightly on her arm, my eyes looking into hers. They hadn't changed, those eyes. Soft, large, brown, holding the beauty of the forest in them as they had the day we'd first met, when I was but the second son of a sachem, and she the daughter of a powaw from a tribe close by. And in all the years since, in all my travels and trials, my joy in looking into those eyes never lessened.

I lay back in the cool, refreshing waters of the river. I had come to scout the best crossing for the main movement of the village and found it quickly, then sent the scouts that had accompanied me back to the camp with orders to make ready to leave at sunrise the next morning. When they did I would lead the sharpest and most concentrated attack yet on the English fort, halting any war parties the English might otherwise send out which might catch the villagers in the vulnerable movement along the trails. Although well worn, the trails between tribes were narrow, dangerous places, especially for a village made up of women, children, and old men.

The attack would not bring a victory over the English army. If that were to come, and many Indians believed it never would, it would be at a future time, with more warriors and less to defend. For now, I must be content with the numerous raids on towns and sharp, if futile, attacks on the fort at Monthaup. I had spent years cajoling, convincing, even pleading with other tribes to join me.

I felt many would join me once the fire of battle was begun, even as the young warriors from those tribes joined me now.

Now I had finally struck the spark. I would know soon if my years of preparation would let that spark catch hold and become a fire – a fire I hoped would sweep across the land until it reached the very edge of the sea itself.

Brookfield – August, 1675

The horses idly stretched their necks down, pulling the deep green grass from the ground in front of them as their riders, thirty of them, looked around the small, grassy clearing and along the trail, vainly searching for the Nipmuck Indians who were supposed to meet them.

"You're certain this was the place?" Captain Edward Hutchinson asked.

"I am. I told Muttawmp to expect us this day, by this hour. He agreed to meet here to discuss peace," said Ephraim Curtis. Curtis had found the Nipmuck sachem only after long days of searching. The traditional Nipmuck villages had been abandoned and new camps formed, as they were in times of war. This had concerned Curtis. But Muttawmp had eagerly greeted Curtis when he'd arrived, and then agreed to these talks, convincing Curtis of his sincerity in his words of peace.

So Hutchinson, a local leader who'd dealt with the Nipmucks for years, had been sent to sue for peace, accompanied by thirty booted and helmeted horsemen to help convince Nipmuck leaders that peace was in their best interest. This was no local, rag-tag militia unit, like the one chasing Philip down south, but a company of some of the most rugged soldiers in the colony, sent from Boston specifically for this mission.

"What are they saying?" Hutchinson asked Curtis, pointing to the three Indian guides accompanying them, who now spoke quietly but in evident excitement to Curtis.

"They say many men have marched over this ground in the last few days. They believe it is a bad sign, that the men are gathering for war." Hearing this, the soldiers stared around the woods uneasily.

"Bahh, they are wrong," Hutchinson spat. "I know these Nipmucks better than they do themselves. They've worked my farm for years. They've worked for us all in these parts. They've always been hard workers and, more to the point, trusted workers. Many have joined the Church. They'd not turn against their friends of so many years just because that blasted King Philip causes a little trouble down south. Let's ride on. I wager we'll find them up ahead, waiting for us with the best of intentions." He spurred his horse on. "Forward men."

The Boston men were less eager to follow, but the men from the village of Brookfield, which lay a short ways back down the trail, reassured them that the captain knew of what he spoke. They all knew the Indians here, and were certain war was the last thing they wanted. They'd be looking for a chance to make peace.

Encouraged by the Brookfield men's assurances, the troops kicked their horses forward and continued down the trail as it wound around a hill to their right, skirting the edges of a swamp on the left.

The swamp was still damp, even in the August heat, and Muttawmp's moccasins filled with the water as he silently crept to where Matoonas peered through the dense, grassy bushes. Down the trail the tramp of horses' feet could be heard.

"They are coming,' Matoonas whispered to him.

"Did you place warriors behind them, to cut off the retreat?"

"As you instructed."

"Good. As they come along this part of the path, they will be forced to go along one at a time. When the center of the column gets to where we are now, I will give the signal."

They went silent again as the horsemen approached. All that could be heard was the rustle of birds above, and the steady drone of mosquitoes flying above the swamp. Not a sound came from the three hundred warriors arranged in a three sided box around the Englishmen, with a fourth side being provided by the steep, bare hill.

The first horseman slowed to a walk, peering into the dense, bushy growth to his left. Muttawmp gazed directly into the Englishman's eyes, and wouldn't have been surprised if the English soldier saw him in return, but he did not. He continued to look around at the terrain as he rode down the trail, followed closely by the rider behind him, their shiny helmets occasionally glinting in the sun.

Muttawmp gazed down the line of riders. His scouts had counted thirty, and he counted to the fifteenth, still down the trail, but now in sight. Muttawmp silently and carefully pulled back the hammer on his gun, locking it into place with a faint click. He watched the man he had chosen to die ride up the trail. He was a short, stout man, his thick legs thrust out by the width of the horse beneath him.

He drew closer and closer, until he rode directly in front of Muttawmp. The Englishman turned his head to scan the hill. Muttawmp rose silently from where he stood, leveled his flintlock, and took aim at the broad chest of the soldier. At that instant the soldier's gaze turned back to the swamp, and for one, fleeting instant his eyebrows rose in surprise as he spied the Indian standing alone, and saw a small puff of smoke rise from the end of the gun.

The soldier's horse reared as the impact of the ball carried the man off its back. But the sound of him hitting the ground was lost in the thunder of the volley which now roared out towards the hill and echoed back.

All along the line men fell, some with the ripping impact of a musket ball, others from being thrown from their horse as the animals panicked at the sound of so much massed gunfire.

Screams of agony followed the thunder, then shouts of command as captains and sergeants attempted to restore order to the troop. At the far end of the line some riders started to retreat the way they had come, only to be met with a second, lesser clap of thunder which again tore into both them and their horses.

The gunfire became more ragged now, as Indians hidden in the swamp and bushes fired as they reloaded. Meanwhile those Englishmen still unhurt from either shot or fall gathered together along the path and on the hill at their backs. They started to return fire as best they could, but they were stuck out in the open, while the Indians remained hidden in the swamp and bushes, and the English shots, if they hit anything, failed to lessen the amount of lead being sent at them.

Sensing the only retreat left was up the steep cliff behind them, Captain Thomas Wheeler, assuming command as Hutchinson lay wounded from the first volley, ordered the men to scramble to the top as best they could. None had to be told a second time and instantly almost two dozen men, a few dragging wounded comrades, urged their horses upwards. The animals pawed and stumbled their way up the rocky cliff, some having to be almost pulled up the slope by the riders who tumbled from them. Those men, reins in one hand, grasped and clawed at the ground with the other, ignoring cuts and bruises appearing with every step, feeling instead the whizzing musket balls behind them, pushing them upwards.

Seeing that the main force of the English was getting away, despite the rocky climb, Muttawmp ordered his warriors forward. But now the terrain which had been their ally in the first minutes of battle became their foe. The line of attack turned ragged and straggled because of the rocks, the dead and dying horses, and the bodies of the dead soldiers. As they reached the bottom of the hill, the attack became even more difficult as they too had to claw and grasp their way up the step slope while being fired upon from above by the English soldiers, volleys which become more effective as the Indians came into the open.

Knowing the English could not now be destroyed with a frontal attack, Muttawmp sent Matoonas up the sides of the cliff to outflank the enemy at the top.

Matoonas moved quickly with a few dozen warriors, but by the time they reached the summit the English soldiers had remounted and escaped down a barely visible path on the rear side of the hill.

Matoonas stepped to the crest of the cliff and spotted Muttawmp at the bottom, still organizing the warriors for attack.

"They have run," Matoonas yelled, partly to Muttawmp, but also to all the warriors. "Like scared rabbits, they have scampered off to the safety of their homes."

"Then let us go show them that their homes are also no longer safe for them," yelled Muttawmp in triumph.

As what remained of the mounted troop hurried on down the indistinct path that led, at least in a general direction, to Brookfield and the garrison, they heard behind them the bloodcurdling victory yell of three hundred ecstatic warriors.

Captain Wheeler, still in charge despite a musket ball in his shoulder, concentrated his mind on the measures to be taken at Brookfield for the town's defense, trying at the sae time to squelch all thoughts of what fate awaited the eight brave men they had left bhind. The morning's hope of peace had been replaced by the afternoon's reality of war.

I arrived at Wenimisset, the fort constructed by the Nipmucks, on the fourth day of the siege of Brookfield, accompanied by fifty warriors, their wives and children. I immediately went into council with Muttawmp, Matoonas, and the other sachems who had joined in the battle. They told me of the victory over the mounted troop on the first day of battle.

"You have done well, extremely well, Muttawmp. As have your warriors, who have proved themselves both brave and dignified." I praised. The assembled leaders, even though used to respect from others, were visibly pleased.

"Now we must use this victory to best advantage," I continued after allowing a moment to let the gathered men enjoy my praise.

"Let me tell you of our efforts to finish the victory," Muttawmp said. "All of Brookfield is now holed up in a single home. Couriers sent to bring help have been killed. Except for the garrison, all houses and buildings have been put to the torch, as have their fields of corn and grain. We have gathered their cattle for our own use.

"We continue to lay siege to their remaining fort. Several attempts have been made to force them out with fire, though they have not yet been successful. One attempt, made with a wagon carefully built to be rolled to the side of the house while in flame, only failed because of a sudden rainstorm. But we will prevail, of that let there be no doubt."

"And that is good," I nodded, not wanting to downplay the efforts of the warriors, "But that is not the advantage I speak of. You have won a great victory over the English soldiers, a victory many said could not be won. The greatest use of the victory lies not against the English, but with the Mohegans, the Niantics, and especially the Narragansetts. We must quickly spread the news of this victory to those who might become our allies."

I could see that Muttawmp, flush with the victory he had planned and led, disagreed with me, although out of respect to my leadership he presented his argument quietly.

"It seems to me," he said, and looked around the wigwam for support, "that we should finish this battle alone. The Narragansetts have never been our friend. We have fought them many times - hard, bitter fights of which stories are still told about the campfire. Why should we let them now come to our side? The soldiers we killed were from Massachusetts, the strongest of the colonies. If we can beat Massachusetts, why should we seek the help of our enemy, the Narragansetts?"

There was a low murmur around the council fire as the sachems debated among themselves the merits of Muttawmp's words. Indeed I was well aware the Narragansetts had never been trustworthy. Conflict with other tribes was common.

But I knew I must start bringing the sachems around to my view of the situation.

"Your victory over the Massachusetts troops was indeed praiseworthy, but do not be fooled by it. Massachusetts will not sit by and let this defeat stand by itself. More troops will march. And not only from Massachusetts, but from Plymouth, and from Connecticut. If pressed, even the Rhode Islanders will join them to fight us."

"Why?" Muttawmp asked, truly confused. "Why should the Plymouth men care if we fight with Massachusetts men? It is not their affair. Why should they come to their side? The Narragansett would not come to ours."

I slapped my hand on my thigh. "There - you have stated our challenge. You are right. In most circumstances the Narragansett would not come to our aid. For the Algonquin people the fight of one tribe is not the fight of another. The matter is settled honorably, between warriors of each tribe. But what have we learned in the last fifty years, if not that the English ways are so different from ours? And that they will not tolerate ways different from their own, even amongst others?

"Understand this. The English will come together. Despite their differences, they are one people. They might squabble among themselves, but when it comes to us, when it comes to the Algonquin, they will stand as one."

"If they are so strong, would it not make sense to stand with them?" said an older sachem I did not recognize. "Combine our strength with theirs to overcome our old enemies, the Narragansetts?"

"Your wisdom is the wisdom of my father - Massasoit," I said with respect, trying to hide my frustration with such an argument. "It is the wisdom of the ages, handed from one generation to my own, and worthy of consideration." Now I rose, an unusual act around the council fire, but I knew I had to shake up the council, or all that had been gained in the last few weeks could be lost.

"But the wisdom of my father does not consider the ways of the English. They are not another tribe to be adjusted to or accommodated. All of you have people in your villages who remember the time before the white man came to live on our shores. And yet in the short time since their arrival, how much land have they asked of us? And once we have given it, how long was it before they came for more? And if we do not give, how long until they take it from us?

"Who among the old can forget the Disease? Brought by the English in the years before they settled here. We all have heard the stories of that time, of the death that swept through our nations, killing us not one or two at a time, but

destroying whole villages with horrible sickness. Disease brought by the English who themselves are unaffected by it. They settled in the very villages abandoned by our stricken tribes."

The old sachem who had questioned Metacomet now cried out in painful memory. "Will they loose the Disease on us again?"

"They will do what they have to to gain the land they need. They may take no more than their need, but their need grows. To beat them in battle, to kill their soldiers, will only delay them. To join with them against the other tribes will only mean ours will be the last tribe whose land they take, but in the end it will be the same."

"Then what can we do?" cried the old sachem in despair.

I looked around with determination. "The English must be driven from the land. While we still have the ability, we must drive them into the sea!"

There was a cheer of agreement, led mainly by the younger sachems, but echoed by all. I had accomplished what I had hoped, the strength that I felt flow through me when I spoke had flowed again. They were mine now if only for the moment. I had learned early on in my travels and negotiations that, while my influence of speech was strong, it was temporary at best.

"But to do this, to drive them back into the sea, we cannot stand alone," I continued. "The Algonquin nations must come together as one to face the English threat. As long as we are divided and they are united, we will be at their mercy.

"But united, we will stand strong against them. We know the land, we know battle. For all their weapons and armor, they are not true warriors. If we unite, they will not be able to withstand us. That is what your victory has shown. That the English can be beaten. But we must bring the Narragansetts in with us. Then, with a thousand warriors, the English will be at our mercy."

I stood, exhausted, panting to regain my breath, waiting to see the reaction my words had brought. The faces surrounding me turned grim, but I recognized it as the grimness of decision and determination.

"What do we do now?" Matoonas asked after a few moments had passed.

I sat down again, signaling return to council. "I myself will go again to the Narragansetts. I have established many friendly relations among them over the past years. There are many who think this way among them, although their sachems are not yet convinced of its truth. But now, accompanied by a few of your brave warriors to tell of your victory, we will be able to bring them new arguments, and proof of our final success over the English."

"I will come with you," Muttawmp said, standing to show his support.

"No Muttawmp. Although your presence would be felt at the council fire, it will be felt even more if you continue here. You have shown the way in the last few days. Plan more attacks. Continue to show all tribes that the English can be

beaten. Do this, and my mission will become almost unnecessary in the face of your work."

"Where should we attack next?"

"I will leave that judgment to you. You know your warriors and your capabilities."

Muttawmp shook his head in silent acceptance.

It was decided. The line had been drawn. The war had begun. What I had worked for for so long had finally come to pass. The English were on one side of the line. It remained to be seen who would join me on the other.

After the council fire had burned to its ember I drew Matoonas away from the others and walked with him down the trail into the forest.

"I need you to stay with Muttawmp and see that all continues as it should," I said.

Matoonas stopped short. "How could you believe it would not?"

"I have been traveling this path for many years now," I said, allowing my face to show the weariness and strain of long years spent on the trails of New England. "I have walked many miles, and talked around many council fires. When I talk, many agree with what I say. They nod their heads and offer grievances to support my own. Then I leave to talk with another tribe. And when I return, it is as if I had never been there."

"They do not remember?"

"They remember only me, not the arguments I spent so much time explaining to them. And so I start again. This time, the arguments are accepted much more quickly. The grievances they tell me now are ones I told them of the time before, but they are told to me as if they are newly discovered. The second time, their agreement is more emphatic, more deeply held. But then I must leave, and as I do, my arguments leave with me, only to be reintroduced the next time and argued by them the next time. By this slow process are men convinced of the rightness of a cause."

"You think your arguments will leave with you this time?" Matoonas asked. "I do not believe the Nipmuck is so forgetful." He was irritated by what he saw as this slight to the honor of the Nipmuck.

"Not as long as the memory of your great victories stays with them" I soothed. "But pick your next few targets with care. A setback now will make the memory of this victory flee from their minds. We cannot risk that. Not now. Not yet. The time will come to take risks. Huge risks. And I will not shirk from them. But now is not that time. Scout out their weaknesses. The English do not know the forests. Make certain Muttawmp uses that to advantage."

"I have faith in Muttawmp's skill."

"I do not say otherwise. His skill is great. But much of that skill rests on his daring. You must control that daring for now, until we have the Narragansetts with us."

"Why do you not speak to him directly?"

"Muttawmp is a proud man. He will not listen to what he thinks are the commands of others. But he will listen to the advice of those whom he trusts. He will listen to you."

Matoonas understood the wisdom of these words. I had heard that before my arrival there had been grumblings among some of the sachems about the way the young warriors flocked to me. After all, I was hardly a proven warrior. The Wampanoags had never been famed for our military exploits. Whenever called before the English leaders, they had said, Philip had always agreed to whatever terms they had demanded. And to be sure I had, I always explained that the time was not yet ready, that more preparations had to be made before the English were defied.

But it had always been my talk, not my actions, that made me a leader. I had talked to all the leaders, together and separately, for years, telling them that they must prepare for the day when action would come forth.

And Matoonas now saw that this day had come. I had done what I said I would do. My work over the past years to unite all the tribes would be needed now if we were to beat the English. But Matoonas also knew many of the older sachems doubted my leadership, and given the chance, would challenge it.

"I will do as you ask," Matoonas said.

"Bring me a victory," I promised, "and I will bring you a thousand Narragansett warriors."

"You have seen they can be defeated. If the Nipmucks can chase the English army through the forest like rabbits, can the Narragansett warrior not do even more? Could they not attack even the very heart of the English settlements and strongholds? And together with the other tribes of the Algonquin nation, could we not push the white invaders back into the sea from which they came?"

I had spent the last several days arguing this point over and over, at one council fire after another, with both minor Narragansett sachems and the most influential ones. I was tired, my throat sore, my voice faltering now and again. And still the Narragansetts argued.

"The Narragansett have been at peace with the English for years. They have respected our lands, and we theirs. We trade with them in ways that are mutually helpful."

"Helpful? How many of your braves have fallen into drunkenness? How many of your men and women have given up the ways of your ancestors and become 'Christian'? Is this the future you wish for your people?"

"There are those who fall under the ways of the English," the Narragansett sachem agreed. "But they are not strong to begin with. The Narragansett lose no strength in losing them. But we gain strength through our friendship with the English. We have guns and powder. We have warm blankets and medicine."

"Medicine for sickness that was unknown before they came."

"Still," said the old sachem, "the wrongs that have been done to us are ones we have allowed ourselves. What you speak is not reason enough to go against the might of the Englishman. What will be our gain? Why risk our people?"

I silently thanked the old man for his comment, for it allowed me to play upon the strong feelings of the younger tribe members.

"Is that then your answer? You are afraid to go against the English? That itself is proof of the changes in your people. Since when was the Narragansett one to cower in fright?

"The English have taken our lands. They have corrupted our young men. They have decreed that we live under their law. They have stolen our dignity! If another tribe had done this to you, you would be calling for their blood. Why then are the English allowed to do it?"

There was an uneasy silence. I caught the eyes of those I knew still opposed me, trying to stare them into silence. One by one they looked away from my eyes, until my gaze fell upon Canonchet, a sachem well regarded for his military skills and leadership in battle.

"With all respect to you and the grievances you may have suffered at the hands of the English," Canonchet began, "it seems your grievance is between the Wampanoag and the Plymouth men. In our own case, our relations with the Rhode Islanders have not faced the problems you've so eloquently spoken of. And while I do not wish to speak dishonor to our guest, I feel I must urge this council to consider that Philip has been telling us this same tale for years. He has tried again and again to get the Narragansett to join with the Wampanoag against the Plymouth men. Perhaps it is not the Indian that suffers at the hands of the white man, but the Wampanoag. Perhaps, and again, I mean no dishonor to you, but it can't be helped, perhaps the Wampanoag seeks our friendship to protect them against the Plymouth in the same spirit that his own father, Massasoit, sought the help of the Plymouth tribe in order to protect the Wampanoag from us."

There was some laughter now among the same sachems who, only moments before, had avoided my gaze.

"When the English grow so strong they feel they can move against the might of the Narragansett, then we might be persuaded to come to the aid of our weaker brothers," Canonchet concluded. "But do not ask us to finish a battle you started."

The council members began to leave. I could not regain their attention without pleading for them to listen, and to do that would play into the very arguments of Canonchet.

But I knew what I must do. Canonchet was the key. As long as he opposed me, the Narragansett would stay out of the war. If he could be convinced, the others would follow. I waited as the sachems headed from the wigwam, then followed Canonchet, coming up beside him once he was alone.

"May I speak with you?" I said.

"Of course, old friend," Canonchet said. I could not tell whether Canonchet was sincere in his use of the word "friend".

"Why do you oppose me?" I asked bluntly.

"I prefer peace to war," said Canonchet simply, so simply I found it hard not to accept it as truth.

"Even if the peace is an undignified one?"

Canonchet pondered this for a moment. "No. I would not accept an undignified peace. But that is not what the Narragansetts have."

"It is what the Wampanoags have."

"Then you have no choice but to fight."

"And you have no choice but to join us. For the fight of the Wampanoag is the fight of all the Algonquin peoples. For whether the fight is fought today, or put off until tomorrow, the fight will come."

"I do not believe that."

"You see peace with the English?"

"I see co-existence. I see the English living on their lands, and us living on ours."

"And no conflicts?"

"Of course there will be conflicts. There will always be conflicts between two different peoples. Just as there have been conflicts between the Wampanoag and the Narragansett, or the Narragansett and the Mohegan."

"And the Pequod? Will there be conflict with the Pequod?"

Canonchet went silent at the mention of this once fierce people, then said quietly, "The Pequod are no more."

"Because of the English. They were in the way of the English, and the English destroyed them. The Pequod should be a warning to you. That is what will happen to us all."

"The Pequod were an unbending people. They took offence too easily. They were too proud. They threatened the very existence of the Englishmen. That is what drove the English to destroy them. And now you threaten the Englishman's existence. Let the Pequod be a warning to you, Metacomet."

We walked in silence. Canonchet argued well, and I found it hard to counter him, even though I knew him to be wrong. But I couldn't let Canonchet get away without more effort.

"The English, Canonchet, are not like the Algonquin. They do not see themselves as separate tribes. You spoke of the Wampanoag conflict with the Plymouth men, and indeed it was the Plymouth men who most directly aggrieved us. Yet when we attacked, when war came, it was not only the Plymouth men who came against us. Massachusetts also sent their armies. And Connecticut offered theirs. They hold together as one nation, despite their differences. I say the Algonquin must do the same."

Canonchet stopped and turned directly to me. "You speak with a certainty I cannot see. You argue well, and I have no doubt you sincerely believe your own arguments. But you must know I believe mine. Of course I cringe at the ways of the English, at the way they promote idleness and drunkenness among our people. But there is also much to be learned from them. If we have cooperation between our peoples, both will become strong."

"But it cannot happen," I argued. "Just as the English see their fates as one, so they view the Indian as a single people. War has begun. The English will not stop to decide whether it is a Wampanoag or a Narragansett they kill. All they know is you are not one of them. The war will engulf you, whether you wish it or not." I was playing my final card now, and Canonchet knew it.

"Now you overstate your case, Metacomet. Already messengers from Massachusetts have come to our councils and assured us that the war is not one against us all. They have asked our cooperation in bringing it to an end."

"Will they receive it?"

"As I told them, the affairs of the Wampanoag are not our affairs. As we will not join with you on making war on the English, neither will we join the English in stopping you from what you feel you must do."

"And the English response?"

"They were disappointed we would not join them. But," Canonchet said firmly, with an emphasis meant to cut off further argument, "they were content to accept our reasons."

"There were no other terms?"

"No," Canonchet said, but, I knew he was lying. Other Nipmuck leaders who were sympathetic to me had told me of Canonchet's dilemma. There were other terms the Narragansett had been forced to accept under the English agreement. No help to the Wampanoags and Nipmucks meant the Narragansetts would turn over to the English any Wampanoag or Nipmuck who entered Narragansett lands. Under the agreement Canonchet was bound to turn me over to them even as I stood here, arguing for help. But I'd heard the Narragansett sachem considered this term merely a sop to the English messengers, meant to assure them of Narragansett neutrality. Neither side, Canonchet thought, expected the agreement to be carried out to that extent. Also, he knew that feelings for me among his own Narragansett, while still controlled, ran high. To turn me over, or any warrior fighting the English, would only cause what he had promised the English would not happen. The tribe would join me, even with the opposition of the sachems. The game of leadership in the Algonquin world, Canonchet and I both knew, required a keen sense of balance.

We walked in silence. But before reaching the village camp, Canonchet turned again to me.

"What will be your path now?"

"The war will continue," I said firmly. "There can be no turning back. The time is here, whether you recognize it or not."

"Other tribes may still join you," Canonchet said, expressing neither hope nor encouragement, just a fact.

"None with the strength of yours," I said, but even as I said it, I was struck by a thought so unexpected, its very appearance silenced me.

"Your face shows your spirit, Metacomet," Canonchet observed. "You have another argument for me?"

"No. I have argued you with all that I care to at this time," I responded, not wishing to share my idea with a man I could not fully trust. "But I will be back. We'll see if a few more victories don't change your mind."

"It will take more than a few small victories to change our minds," Canonchet warned. "It will take a small earthquake."

"Perhaps that," I said, turning and walking away from Canonchet as I said it, for emphasis, "is what I will give you."

Deerfield - October, 1675

The fall harvest around Deerfield had been a tense one. Shortly after the outbreak of hostilities the normally peaceful Pocumtucks had ambushed a small party coming back from church. Although losses had been light, one man killed and two homes burned, the incident had shown this small settlement just how vulnerable they were out here along the northern banks of the Connecticut River. Thirty miles downriver lay Springfield, the only town of any real size nearby. One hundred hard, overland miles separated them from Boston, their capital. The only town farther up the river, Northfield, had already been evacuated.

After the ambush soldiers were dispatched to punish the tribe. But despite diligently searching the nearby hills, no trace of the Pocumtucks could be found. It was if they had disappeared.

But raids on cattle and foodstuffs continued, confirming the Pocumtucks presence. There'd been several sharp skirmishes, and a handful of men on both sides had been killed. Now rumors were circulating that a large number of Indians had gathered in the hills surrounding the town. One rumor had King Philip in the area waiting to pounce. Taking no chances, the English had ordered Deerfield also be evacuated. Captain Lathrop now came with eighty troops to oversee the evacuation, and to help with the harvesting of the fields before they left.

"Ahh," shrugged off burly John Townsend, a middle-aged man who was gathering hay into the nearby wagon. "If everybody who has professed to see that scalawag in the town were right, there'd have to be a dozen of him."

"But I heard Sergeant Oakes say so himself," sad Jonas, Townsend's fifteen year old son. "He says he knows for a fact that another two hundred Indians marched into the hills there, and Philip was at the head of them."

"Shows you what he knows," Townsend grunted as he pitched another forkful of hay into the wagon. "It's common knowledge that for all his bragging, King Philip is nothing but a blowhard coward. Frankly I hope its true he's here. 'Cause if he's here, you can be sure no fighting is going to happen."

"Hope you're so certain of your facts when King Philip slips up behind you and cuts your throat."

"Damn my eyes, Oakes. When did you get here? Nearly scared me out of my skin!"

"Been here nearly an hour."

"All the time on top of that hay wagon, I bet. Sleeping."

"Not sleeping. Protecting you and the boy here from the Indians." Oakes raised his gun above the hay for Townsend to see.

"All's I know is, if you're so bent on protecting us, how come your hair's all full of hayseed? Looks to me like you've been sleeping," Townsend groused. But it was good natured. He appreciated that troops had been sent to the community, even if they did have a penchant for lounging. Just the presence of a hundred or so well-armed men should have a calming effect on the Pocumtucks.

"As long as you're here, why don't you help bring in this field of hay? The faster we get it in, the less time we're sitting out in the middle of this field pretending to be target practice for King Philip."

"Afraid if I was working the hayfield, I mightn't be diligent in my guarding duties. And one has to stay diligent. That Philip is a crafty one." Oakes said these words for the benefit of Jonas, who looked at him with a mixture of awe and disbelief.

"You ever seen Philip? Up close?" Jonas asked.

"Many times. Of course, that was before the war."

"What did he look like?" Despite all the talk about Philip in the last few months, Jonas hadn't been able to obtain a real accurate description.

"Big man," Oakes said, clearly enjoying the attention he was getting, and planning to make the most of it. "With long black hair and beady little eyes that stare out at you like the very depths of hell itself. One of his hands is scarred bad. Story I heard tell is that he stuck it into a fire when he was a youngster, on a dare. Kept it there until the flesh burned. That's why some say he's the devil incarnate. Day I saw him he was wearing nothing but an old militia jacket and a ragged piece of cloth over his cod."

"Oakes, I'll have none of that talk in front of the boy," bellowed Townsend. "It's bad enough you're filling his head with these tales, never mind turning them into smut."

"Just trying to tell the boy the truth. Course, if you don't believe me you can just go up there and check out what he looks like for yourself." Oakes pointed to the hill that sloped steeply up behind them. "More'n likely Philip's up there right now."

"Gosh, Pa, I'm scared. We'd best get back to the village right now," Jonas said, then blushed as Oakes rolled back on the hay laughing.

"Don't listen to him, son," Townsend said, jamming his fork back into the next pile of hay. "He knows nothing more about all this than you or I. But I at least know this, if we don't get this hay in to feed our cattle, we'll die of hunger this winter. Now that's something you can be sure of. More sure than all those Indians Oakes thinks are hiding out up that hill." He pointed up the hill to Oakes' Indians with his pitchfork.

Up that hill, Muttawmp watched the pitchfork. He turned to Matoonas, who squatted beside him as they studied the scene below. It was a scene being repeated in field after field north of the village. Dozens of wagons would be filled with hay. Still others were being filled with the belongings of the thirty families still left in the village. All of these wagons would then clamber onto the road heading south, surrounded by armed soldiers, making the trek to the relative safety of Northampton.

"Why not fall on them as they work in the fields?" Matoonas asked. It seemed the perfect opportunity, men scattered throughout in small bunches, hundreds of yards apart. Two dozen could be attacked and killed, then a main attack could be launched. It could be Brookfield all over again.

"If they were leaving their fields to go back to their village and garrison houses, we would. But that is not our best opportunity. Better to let them work. Meanwhile we will go prepare."

The wagon train moved slowly down the rough but passable road to Northampton, now but six miles distant. The sun shone brightly, without a trace of the chill that often accompanied an early fall day in the valley. A few trees showed the bright oranges and reds that would soon envelop them all, but green remained the predominant color.

John Townsend rode in his wagon near the end of the line, with Jonas at his side, flintlock across his knees. Sergeant Oakes road next to them on a small gray pony, his legs hanging off the sides like two sticks.

"Ought to get yourself a real horse," Townsend said with a light hearted tone he did not feel. It wasn't easy to abandon your home. "Why old Nell here could ride rings around that pup." Townsend snapped the reins on old Nell, whose reaction to the sting of the leather was small, if indeed there was any at all.

"That old plow horse? I think the speed it's pulling that wagon is about as fast as it's ever going to go," Oakes said, a twinkle in his eye. He for one was glad to leave Deerfield behind. There were more men in Northampton, under Captain Mosely and Captain Treat. Not that eighty well armed troopers couldn't hold off any Indian attack, but it had been so quiet the last few days something didn't seem right to him. He was just as glad to have the hayfields behind him.

"Keep hold of that gun, Jonas. No telling when an Indian might pop out of the ground in front of you."

"Mind you Oakes, stop scaring the lad," Townsend groused. There was enough to be scared of without Oakes adding to it. But Jonas clenched the gun a little tighter, and Townsend noticed his son run his finger lightly over the trigger. "Careful there son, don't have it agoin' off without aiming it somewhere but at your Pa."

"Sorry," Jonas laughed nervously. "I reckon I am a little on the edge."

"Don't blame you, the way Oakes talks. That's the trouble with soldiers. If they aren't fighting, they got nothing to do but talk about it, whether it be true or. . . Ho, there, Nell."

Townsend pulled back on the reins, and the big horse clip-clopped to a halt, but not before coming up against the back of the wagon in front of her making her pull to the left. Jonas felt the wagon fall to his father's side.

"If that don't beat all," Townsend said, getting down from the wagon's bench. "The twist snapped the axle. This will take a bit to fix." He looked up at the offending wagon driver ahead. "What's got into your head man, stopping like that?"

The driver of the wagon in front of them turned over his shoulder. "Not my fault. Wagon in front of me did the same thing. Whole line's stopped. Seems there's a log down ahead in the road. It'll take them a few minutes to chop it and move it out. Hold tight."

"Hold tight my ass," Townsend muttered, and Jonas stared at his father. He'd never heard him curse before.

"C'mon Oakes, make yourself useful for once. Get down off that little goat of yours and help me with this axle. I got a spare in the bed. Oakes? You gone deaf?"

Oakes heard, but ignored him. He was glancing around the forest, pulling his pony back around as he stared into the edges of trees. A log down in the road? Sure it happened. But why now? Why here? Oakes looked, and then he found what he was looking for.

"Aww, Jeeesus. Jonas get your. . ." But Jonas never heard the rest of Oakes statement. Instead he saw Oakes face explode in a red and white mess of blood and bone, and only then, an instant later, did Jonas hear the explosion of hundreds of guns, all fired at once.

"Ambush!" Jonas heard his father yell as he tore the gun from Jonas's hands and pushed Jonas into the rough dirt below the wagon bed. Jonas heard the crack of his father's gun, and then other guns along the line of the wagons. He hid his face in his arms as the sounds of yelling and cursing rose all around him, mixed with the high pitched squeals of the Indian attack that came from all sides. He heard a musket ball thud into the earth next to him, felt the earth it kicked up fall on him like little, solid raindrops.

He looked up then, but all he could see in the forest's edge was smoke. He heard a scream, closer than the rest, and out of the smoke popped an Indian warrior, his face painted like some fiendish devil out of Jonas' Sunday Bible class, mouth open, hand raised above his head, tomahawk clenched in his fist, bearing down on the wagon.

"Pa!" Jonas yelled, but in the din he barely heard himself. He looked up to see his father level the gun and fire again. He looked back. The Indian fiend lay several feet back from where Jonas has last seen him, still screaming, but now it was a scream of agony as he fingered the hole that had suddenly appeared in his chest.

Jonas was still watching the Indian flop like a caught fish when he felt his collar grabbed from above.

"C'mon, Jonas, we've got to get up to the rest of them."

With his father clutching his collar, the two of them ran up the road, ducking behind wagons, horses, and anything else that might provide cover, up to where a small group of soldiers had managed to pull into a circle. When they reached it, his father threw him roughly behind some sacks of grain that had been tossed into the center to some sort of protection from the lead balls and wooden arrows that came from the sky like a winter blizzard. Jonas huddled down behind the sack's relative safety and tried to calm himself. But the sight of Oakes exploding face came leaping back into his mind. He leaned over and vomited, with deep, heaving gasps of breath. The smell of it stung his nostrils as he leaned his head up against the sacks of grain. But it would be hours before he could move away from it.

From a small rock outcropping that hung above the road Muttawmp impassively watched the battle unfold beneath him. The initial surprise had been complete, the confusion brought on by the downed log adding to the confusion of the train. Their initial volley had downed two dozen soldiers, at least. Even more had fallen in the next few minutes as they attempted to regroup and fortify.

Now, fifteen minutes into the battle, the small band of soldiers had done the only thing they could do. They'd formed a tough defensive circle made up of wagons, horses, and in one small part of the circle, bodies of the other soldiers.

"They fight bravely," Matoonas said of the Englishmen below them.

"They fight bravely because they have no other way left to them," Muttawmp said contemptuously, then added, "And they will continue to fight bravely until they are dead."

As the day passed, Muttawmp guided his warriors skillfully, launching well coordinated attacks against the Englishmen's position, each time killing a few more defenders while suffering almost no losses of his own.

The toll on the English defenders grew, both in lives and in hope. Half of the men who had survived the initial ambush were now dead or dying, and there were no signs of the attack weakening. Ammunition was running low. Destruction was imminent. But still they methodically poured in the powder, tamped down the wadding, dropped in the musket ball, tamped again, leveled their musket, and shot when, and only when, they could spot a target.

Muttawmp, joined by Matoonas who had coordinated and lead the first attacks, was again scouting the situation from the rock outcropping.

"A strong blow now and victory will be complete," Matoonas observed. "And a great victory it will be. Metacomet will be proud."

Muttawmp grunted. "It is not Metacomet who I wish to impress," he said. "It is the Narragansett and the Niantic. Metacomet is right when he says the only way to finally defeat the English is to unite. So we do not fight for Metacomet. We fight for ourselves."

Matoonas considered this for a moment, thinking of a reply, but finally decided such a great victory should not be marred by petty bickering, and remained quiet. He turned his attention back to the scene below as the Nipmuck and Pocumtuck warriors massed for a final blow.

But as the warriors started forward, a loud, sustained crack thundered behind them, to the right of where Muttawmp and Matoonas watched. Several Indians fell, and the rest turned from the small, isolated band of survivors to meet this new challenge. They were met with another volley of gunfire, and then a third, riddling their ranks and causing confusion.

Coming down the trail in a well ordered hurry were troops under the command of Captain Mosely.

The Indians, while still heavily outnumbering the English, were now caught in between the small but well fortified survivors of the wagon train and the onrushing troops of Mosely. Being fired on from both sides, and being vulnerable in their rear, they scampered for safety into the woods and hills.

Seeing the change, Muttawmp sprang from the ledge and ran down the hill, Matoonas chasing after him. They quickly reached the first of the retreating warriors.

"Hold up! Regroup! Victory is ours if we stand and fight," he yelled, grabbing single warriors as they tried to get past him and physically turning them back to the fight. Matoonas did likewise, and soon they had gathered a small group of warriors, all intent on not allowing victory to get away.

Muttawmp sent out a small group to hit the side of Mosely's attacking troopers, waiting a few moments while they put themselves into position, using the time to move other warriors. Others, seeing what Muttawmp was doing, added their guns to the force.

Just below them the advance group of troopers had punched their way through to the beleaguered survivors of the wagon train. A few moments more and the troops would form a strong defensive position.

Muttawmp signaled his warriors forward. With a bloodcurdling scream they streamed out of their positions and threw themselves into the troopers who were raggedly trying to form a defensive line. The fighting became hand to hand, with the knives and cutlasses of the troopers matched against the blows of the Algonquin tomahawks. As each found their mark agonized screams of pain from both Indian and Englishman rose through the valley. The fighting remained face to face before the Indians fell back to regroup.

"You there," yelled one of the newly arrived English soldiers, spying a small form curled up behind sacks of grain. "What are you doing?"

Jonas Townsend crept out from behind the safety of the grain bags. He'd been too scared to even peek out from behind. Instead he had listened to the screams and cries, to the whistles of musket balls, listened for the occasional, comforting sounds of his father's voice through the din. But until now he hadn't come out.

A gruesome sight awaited him. It was Sergeant Oakes exploded face repeated over and over again, in both English and Indian form. Dead bodies lay everywhere, slashed by tomahawks, and ripped open by musket balls. He turned back to the grain bags, heaving up what contents of his stomach still remained. He stayed that way, retching over and over again, until he felt a set of hands on his shoulders and a familiar voice.

"Come along Jonas," his father said. "We're going to fall back to Northampton."

Jonas looked up into his father's face. It was covered with grime, sweat, and blood. He let out a small cry.

"Ehh?" his father said, looking at him, then realized. "None of it's mine, lad, Lord be praised," he said, wiping off his forehead with his sleeve to show. "But it might be if we don't get on down the trail. C'mon. It's hard, I know, but your mother will be waiting on us."

Jonas thought of his mother for the first time this afternoon. He gave thanks to God she had gone to Northampton earlier, and been spared this ordeal. Never again would Jonas ask for exciting tales of the Indian. He'd had his fill. Forever.

The Englishmen began to fall back down the trail towards Northampton, still six miles off. But as they started, the Indians attacked again. With each attack, more Indians joined in the fury. It took all the skill and fortitude of the remaining soldiers to hold them back from the main column.

The next few miles were a hell Jonas had never imagined. Time and time again the Indians attacked the rear, sides, and even the front of the column, springing up from swamps and forests until it seemed to Jonas they came from the ground itself to unleash their silent arrows, or tear into the column with an explosion of guns.

But the weary troopers pressed on, bringing with them what remained of the wagons. With each mile more of them were hurt, wounded, killed. The dead were reluctantly left behind. The rest were slowed down by the added burden of the maimed. Jonas was put to work driving a team of oxen pulling a wagon with a dozen wounded men. Those who weren't mercifully unconscious cried out in pain. Jonas tried to block them out, concentrating instead on keeping the oxen moving forward, towards Northampton and safety.

With four miles left to Northampton, and still another Indian attack launched against them, Jonas began to doubt he would live. In his young life he'd seen death, but never before had he imagined he might be its victim. He felt tears fill his eyes as he conjured up the image of his mother waiting and waiting, then hearing the tragic news.

He heard gunfire in the distance in front of them. More Indians, he thought, but then he saw the mounted troopers of another relief column, this one commanded by Captain Treat. Despite the horror and terror of the day, Jonas couldn't help but break into a wide smile. He might yet live to see his mother.

Not wanting to risk the greatest single victory of the Algonquin over the English with even a minor setback, Muttawmp called off the attack once Treat's men came into view.

The younger warriors came to him, begging, pleading to be allowed to continue. Their faces were smeared with blood, some from battle, and some as a badge of honor, spread on after a kill. They had tasted blood and wanted more.

Muttawmp raised his hand for silence. "My brave friends. We have won our victory today. Your actions and deeds will be told over and over again at fires throughout the Algonquin nations. No advantage is to be gained from continuing the pursuit. The English have given us their village. We have defeated not one, but two of their armies. No more will the English think he can dictate his law to the Algonquin."

The warriors cheered and yelled their approval of Muttawmp's words. Near him Matoonas joined in the cheers. He watched Muttawmp with awe. The Nipmuck sachem had planned and carried out a battle only a few weeks ago Muttawmp himself had said was impossible.

It was a victory not even Metacomet would have dared dream of.

"Surely the Narragansett will change their minds after this," Matoonas said with disbelief to me. "We have demonstrated our superiority over the English. It is as you have said, they can be beaten if we all join together."

The two of us sat on the rocky outcropping where Muttawmp and Matoonas had overseen the ambush of the wagon train. Below us, unaware of two sachems high above them, a strong troop of Englishmen collected the bodies of the English dead, carefully watching for any Indians that might be in the area. Sixty four bodies would be laid into the wagons they had brought with them.

"The Narragansett believe this is still a war between the Wampanoag and Nipmuck against Massachusetts and Plymouth."

"But it is no longer just the Wampanoag and the Nipmuck. The Pocumtuck and Quabog have joined us. Others are coming."

"The Narragansett care nothing about those tribes," I said. "And compared to the Narragansett, those tribes are nothing. They have no great warriors, no great victories in battle. The Narragansett say the English fight these tribes because they are weak. They believe the English will dare not attack the Narragansett."

"Do they not remember the Pequods? A mighty nation also, but gone now."

"They scoff at the Pequods, saying their might was overestimated. Even the more reasonable among them, men such as Canonchet, say the Pequod were beaten more by the Disease, that the war only finished what the Disease began. Times have changed, they say."

"Without the Narragansett, what chance have we?" Matoonas asked in anguish. I turned to him, allowing a smile to play on my lips. "As long as we continue winning battles such as this one," I said gesturing to the wagons that were now heading back to Northampton with their grisly cargo, "our chances are those of the porcupine against the bear. We might not defeat them, but we can prick them hard and survive. And then, perhaps, the Narragansett might see more than the trinkets the English give them to keep the peace."

The next few weeks were spent much as I said. Hadley was attacked and abandoned. Westfield was also forced to evacuate. Even Springfield, the largest English town in the western part of the colonies, was furiously attacked and, although this didn't force its abandonment, the fields of corn and hay were burned, and the only grist mill capable of milling flour in the valley was destroyed. Almost all of the homes in town were put to the torch. Except for the garrisons, we left Springfield a smoky, blackened remnant.

Indian tribes surrounding Springfield flocked to my camp. And it was to me that they pledged their loyalty, my reputation as the leader of the war firmly established, even though Muttawmp and Matoonas planned and carried out most of the raids and battles.

Throughout New England other tribes and leaders now undertook similar raids, although less ambitious in scope. Targets - outlying, little fortified areas that could not be reached quickly by troops - were carefully chosen. But only with the largest warrior armies did we dare engage the English armies directly.

And those armies were getting more active. As we grew bolder and our raids more frequent, colonists demanded their governments take action against the Algonquin. Armies were raised and put into the field, but we warriors stayed elusive, attacking quickly and fiercely, then melting off in the swamps and woods before the English army could search us out and fight us.

I lingered near Deerfield, sending messengers and ambassadors out to gather news and urging still other tribes to join me. Much of the effort was directed at the Narragansett, but despite increased incidents between them and the English, an uneasy peace remained in place.

Wootonekanuske joined me at Deerfield, establishing as best she could a comfortable wigwam for us and our son.

"It is not easy," she said to me one morning after a particularly cold night. The leaves surrounding their wigwam carried a hint of frost, but the fire she stirred up from the night's embers made the wigwam warm, if smoky. "Food is growing short. As more warriors join us, it eats further into the winter's supply. Shelter is also scarce. Many slept under the stars last night without even a blanket."

"I understand," I said wearily. I had spent much of my time the last several days organizing and sending off delegations to other tribes with the express purpose of bringing in more food for the winter. I had given others the task of gathering what food stores were in the area. Still others I sent hunting and trapping and fishing. In winter food would become more valuable than gunpowder.

"The war now shifts from one of battle to one of survival for both us and the English. As we have burned their fields and mills, so they have driven us from our fields and hunting grounds. The winter will be hard, but we must survive it."

"I did not mean to offend, my husband," Wootonekanuske said, bringing me a small wooden bowl full of broth made from boiled chestnuts and the bone marrow of a fox. I slurped at the hot mixture, savoring the warmth the watery broth spread through my insides.

"You only speak the truth, telling me of conditions I must know." I replied. "Tell me this? Are the people prepared for a winter of shortages? Do they understand its reason?"

Wootonekanuske's lips pursed. I knew she would report as truthfully as she could. She, more than most, understood my need for good information.

"Right now the talk is strong and proud. Warriors say they will fight on even if it means they are nothing but bones. But once the cold and hunger of winter are upon them for any length of time, I suspect their ardor will desert them. The winter will separate out those who believe from those who want no more than an excuse to plunder."

"But which is the stronger party? How will they separate?"

"The answer to that, my husband, is not yet set. Many who believe do so only as long as they still glimpse a chance for victory. The stronger that chance appears, the more who will last the winter in your camp and be ready for the spring battles."

I sipped out the last of the broth, then set down the wooden bowl in front of me. Wootonekanuske waited patiently for my thoughts, even as I sorted through them in my head.

"You see the same things as I," I said. "Hope must be held out to these men. Hope that I cannot as yet promise."

"Are the Narragansett no closer to joining us?"

"Closer yes, but not close enough. If we can last the winter then I believe in the Spring they will join us, whether led by their sachems or pushed by their younger warriors who already are eager to fight with us. But the burden is ours to last the winter, and to do that, as you have said, there must be hope. And it must be a hope stronger than that the Narragansett may join us."

"You must go to the Mohawks," she stated more than asked. We'd discussed it before, although never outside our wigwam.

I nodded. "If the Narragansetts do not join us, we need another tribe to go into battle with us. The Mohawks are as strong as the Narragansett. Stronger in fact."

"But they have never had alliances with any tribe of the Algonquin nation. Will hatred of the white man alone be enough to have them join with us now?"

"It may. They have fought often with the English at Albany. At the very least I need them to renew their attacks there, to prevent assistance coming to the colonies we fight against. But even if I cannot, there is a more important benefit that simply negotiating with Mohawks will bring."

"What is that?"

"Hope."

I missed Matoonas. I missed Wootonekanuske. But neither could be spared from the preparations and plans that continued along the banks of the Connecticut. I missed their counsel, wanted to talk to them, if only to speak out my own thoughts as I negotiated with the Mohawk.

Not that I had come alone. I was accompanied by most of my own Wampanoag warriors, four hundred men in all. It had been felt by the war council that this would be a suitable display to the Mohawks, that the presence of the very warriors who had begun the war against the English would help further negotiations.

And it had. I had been welcomed with much ceremony and celebration. A feast was held in my honor, with dances and songs. Over the soothing smoke of tobacco the deeds and battles of King Philip, as the Mohawks insisted on calling me, were spoken of with enthusiasm. Great victories, whether mine or not, were attributed to my skill and leadership by the Mohawk, who explained they had heard of my triumphs through their dealing with the English at Albany.

"Yours is a name that brings fear into the eyes of the English coward," said an old warrior the other called One-eye, due to a terrible scar forcing his left eye permanently closed. One-eye spoke loudly, affected by the liquor many were drinking freely, liquor gained, they told me, from a raid held only the night before a small outpost a few miles from this very council fire.

"Say 'Philip' to the English and they try to pretend contempt, but their fear is a stench they cannot escape. To have them in such fear you must be a great warrior, and have won great victories." One-eye stumbled a bit, catching himself on my shoulder and leaning into my face, assaulting me with whiskey-laden breath. "You must be one hell of a scoundrel."

I winced, wriggled out from his grasp, and turned my gaze back upon the others gathered around the council fire, who had not drunk any of the English spirits.

"Our victories have been great, it is true," I said, knowing I had to make the most of what we had accomplished. "The English were driven before us like rabbits before a pack of dogs. They scampered through the bushes with their tails ahead of their legs." The warriors laughed, and One-eye slapped his thigh so hard he winced in pain, then laughed again. I continued.

"But as the rabbit scampers before the dog, so does he ultimately escape by burrowing into the ground, where a dog cannot get him. So do the English retreat to their forts. They cower in them like rabbits, afraid to come out for fear of the Algonquin. They screech and howl, and burrow even further.

"And this is why I come to you. Your fierceness and bravery in battle is well known. Indeed, many of my own nation quake at the sight of your warriors coming down from the hills. Your strength is also feared. We need your strength to join with our own to destroy the white man once and for all. It is not enough that we push them back into their forts. We wish now to push them into the sea. To do that, we need your warriors."

I peered into the shadows around the fire. The arguments, so stale and old to me were new to the Mohawk, and I saw interest in more than a few faces. But most were still unmoved.

"Why should we cross the hills to your fight, and join in your battles?" said one who I had noticed the first day because of his height. I noticed him every night thereafter. He had paid careful attention to what I said, and I had seen other Mohawks glance for his reaction to my statements. He was obviously a well-respected sachem. But until this moment he had not spoken. "We have English of our own to fight. Why leave our homeland and fight your battles?"

"The fight against the white man must be fought by a united Indian nation. I make this promise to you. When we have driven the white man from our shores, we will bring our victorious armies over the hills and drive them from your land also." This was far beyond what I could confidently promise, but the words came out easily and, I think, forcefully.

"Why your battle first?" the tall one continued.

"For the simplest of reasons. We are fighting now. The war is on, the battle begun. We come to you not to help us begin the war, but to help us finish it."

The tall one did not reply, but resumed his passive face and stared again into the council fire embers.

But over the next two weeks little changed with the Mohawks. While respectful of me, the Mohawk leaders gave no hint of joining with us. Finally, growing impatient and anxious about war preparations, I told my hosts I would leave the next day to return to my own land.

The Mohawk leaders solemnly agreed to give further consideration to the words I had spoken. In return I promised to send messengers to keep the Mohawks informed about the course of the war, an offer the Mohawks accepted. Saying they wished to show respect to a great warrior, the Mohawks gave me beaded shirts and carved tobacco pipes, which though I accepted gratefully, I felt were small comfort to show my people on my return.

Finally we were allowed to take our leave of the Mohawks, turning our backs to the banks of the Hudson, and starting on the trails over the high hills that separated the Hudson River tribes from those of the Connecticut Valley.

"Will they join us?" Charles asked me as we prepared camp that night, several miles of our journey behind us.

"No. They will not join us. They do not believe it is their fight, but I still hope they will press the attack on the Englishmen here."

"Then why leave? Why not stay and press that argument?" Charles had been impressed by the Mohawk people, especially the skills of the younger braves he had met. He didn't want to leave too quickly, especially with the cold days of winter upon us.

"It is time to head back to our people. We must plan and prepare. We must use the winter to ready ourselves for the spring battles. I have done what I can with the Mohawks. Sleep now. We have a long trail awaiting us in the morning."

Charles dutifully reclined on his blanket. Soon his breathing turned deep and regular. But I could not sleep. I stared at the stars visible through the smoke hole of the tent.

Neither the Mohawks nor the Narragansetts would be part of the force I would lead against the English in the Spring. Instead of all out war against the English, a carefully laid plan of continued raids and attacks on outlying communities would have to be substituted. I knew this could be continued for years if necessary. But what good would it do in the end?

The English had to be attacked at their root. Not only did Deerfield and Springfield need to be attacked, but more settled areas. Lancaster, Medfield, even Boston itself must feel the fear of the flame and iron of the Algonquin. Only then could the English be forced from their land. Our land, I reminded myself. The land of my fathers and forefathers. I would not let it be taken.

But there had to be help. During this winter the plan had become merely one of survival. Then in the spring continued raids and attacks on unfortified outposts. Perhaps the Narragansetts would join us then. Perhaps then even the Mohawks. But that would be then. For now I must put my energies into preserving what I had started.

These thoughts kept sleep from me for several hours, but finally past exertions overtook future worries and I fell into a fitful sleep.

I was awakened by a scream, followed quickly by another, and then a large yell of many men.

I sprang from my blanket, grabbing the loaded gun I kept next to me, searching through the murky light of dawn. I barely spied the lunging figure of a large Indian charging at me, tomahawk held high, mouth open in a high pitched shriek.

I leveled my gun and fired. The Mohawk was lifted backwards in the air, falling into a limp mass not twenty feet away. But others streamed into camp, dozens of them. I grabbed my own tomahawk from next to where I had slept and shook Charles, who was looking around dazed.

"Mohawks!" I yelled. "They are attacking. Get up."

Charles stirred just as I felt a rough hand on my own shoulder, twirling me around. I found myself face to face with One-eye, clenching tightly the wrist I held the tomahawk in.

"So this is who the English fear so mightily?" One-eye asked derisively, raising his knife to strike me. "Imagine the treasures they will give me for the head of King Philip."

But One-eye's expression suddenly melted into surprise, then slipped into nothingness, his knife falling from his hand. Behind him, Charles delivered a second blow from his own knife, twisting the blade as he pushed it into the now lifeless body of the Mohawk. I shook my hand free from One-eye's and, with a brief, thankful grunt to Charles, turned my attention to the scene around me.

The battle was hand to hand, but in almost all of them one Wampanoag warrior took on two or three Mohawks. I quickly saw that continued resistance meant death.

"Retreat!" I yelled, then plunged into the fray, hacking at the exposed backs of the Mohawk warriors, temporarily freeing the Wampanoag they were attacking, and urging the warriors to escape into the forest. I did this for a half dozen of my warriors before I had a dozen Mohawks chasing me. I darted into the forest, tomahawk in one hand, a shiny knife I had picked up in the other, less than six feet ahead of my closest Mohawk pursuer. A gun fired well behind me, and I heard its ball whistle by a few feet to my right.

I leapt easily over a fallen log and heard the Mohawk closest to me stumble. But I did not dare look back. Instead I flew down the trail, imagining myself a rabbit, oblivious to the branches and twigs scratching my face and hands. A few more feet and I left the trail, sliding down a river embankment, pausing at the bottom to glance behind. One Mohawk was half way down the bank. Others were at the top, hesitating. I waited while the one Mohawk slid down out of control, just as I had. As the Mohawk slid towards me, I swung my tomahawk in a mighty, horizontal arc. The unbalanced warrior tried bravely to thrust forward with his own knife, but missed me just as my own blow connected.

The warrior's chest split open like a dried oak, and his scream pierced through the forest. Dropping his weapons he raised his arms to his head to shield any more blows. But I did not strike again. Instead I splashed off across the river towards the other bank. Another musket ball thudded into the hard ground next to me as I reached it, but when I turned again to look at my pursuers they were no longer chasing me. I ran anyway, deeper and deeper into the forest, until I knew even an experienced tracker could not follow me without taking some time.

I sat down on a rock, gasping for breath, replaying in my mind the events of the last few minutes. I saw Mohawks streaming through my camp, slashing my Wampanoags as they lay asleep in their blankets. I saw the brave resistance of those who were able to struggle to their feet. I saw dozens of the bravest men I would ever know fall under the savage blows of the on rushers. I remembered only a handful of faces escaping into the woods, like myself. All I could hope was that they'd gotten as far as I had.

Was this what my revolt against the Englishman had come to? The Narragansetts sitting idly by? The Mohawks seeking to kill me to exploit the very reputation I had gained among the English?

What now lay ahead? A long winter of survival, hoping the force now assembled on the strength of my name would last until the thaws of spring. Hoping that it would not melt away upon the news of this humiliating defeat. Was that what the future held for me?

I leaned back, resting my head against the hardness of the rock. And for the first time since my brother Alexander's death, I wept.

In The Great Swamp-
December, 1675

Canonchet surveyed the stone and earth wall with satisfaction. Beside him Stone-Wall John, so known because of his masonry skill learned while a servant of the Englishman Richard Smith, explained what still remained to be done.

"The outer ring is almost complete. Spikes will be placed all along the top of the wall. Over here," he said, pointing to a still open space at the farthest end of the wall, "will be the entrance, which can only be reached by crossing a single log set across a watered ditch. Even this entry will be protected by two large blockhouses placed to give us crossfire down into it, should it become necessary."

"You have done great work. I wish I could tell you to rest, but I cannot. The work must go faster. Scouts report the armies of the English have come together."

"They have given us no warning of attack," Stone-Wall said. Among the Narragansett, war was always announced to the other side, so that women and children could be removed from the likely scene of battle.

"No," Canonchet agreed. "But I do not trust the English to do so. It is my understanding the army they have gathered is sent to destroy us."

"What has happened? Did you not reaffirm your treaty with them two months ago?"

"They feel Weetamoo's presence among us, with her people, violates that agreement. They say we give aid and comfort to the enemy. This, they say, they will not allow."

"But to attack without giving warning?" Stone-Wall marveled at the indignity of the English. He had led yesterday's delegation from the Pettaquamscutt camp to the battle camp a few miles south of where they stood to question the English intent. The English had fired on them and chased them off. The other warriors had returned to the Pettaquamscutt camp, the English on their heals. But Stone-Wall had broken off from the trail and returned here to oversee the finishing of the defenses. "Where are the warriors now?"

"Encamped at Pettaquamscutt," Canonchet replied. "We will be ready for them. The English do not realize the size of the cat who's tail they are pulling." Canonchet's satisfied smile made Stone-Wall John think that war with the English had been his wish all long. But that was no surprise. In private council Canonchet had always argued that English aggressions, even the least of them, should be resisted. But he had abided by the collected wisdom of the Council, and the Council had chosen to pursue peace.

Now it was the English who asked for war. So preparations begun months before were hastened, including the building of this fortress. It was designed to protect the women, children, and older men of the Narragansett, as well as to be a base of supplies for the coming winter. It was as impressive a sight as Stone-Wall John could remember, even in his time spent among the Englishmen.

The wall he displayed with such pride to Canonchet stood around a five acre square of land, encircling and protecting the dry earth. Inside the wall hundreds of wigwams had been constructed to house and shelter nearly one thousand people who dwelt there. The wigwams were lined inside with baskets of grain and corn, which served two purposes, the first to provide a solid food supply for the winter, and the second to stop the penetration of musket balls, should the need arise.

But the need should never arise because of the fort's greatest strength. While its construction made it virtually impregnable, it location was its best defense.

It sat on the one dry spot of any size for miles around. It lay in the heart of The Great Swamp, a place virtually unknown to the English. The path through the swamp to the fort was twisted and nearly impossible to follow even for Indians who felt comfortable among the swamps. The English, Canonchet knew, hated swamps, considered them evil places, and avoided them at all cost. The English would hesitate to enter the Swamp, and would never delve so far into it in search of the Algonquin.

But still, Canonchet would not find peace until he knew the fortress was complete.

"Hurry, Stone-Wall, I do not want concerns with the safety of the village as I lead my warriors."

Stone-Wall John replied calmly. "The work will be completed in a few days, if the snows do not come. Then it will be impossible to attack. But even now it is impossible. Do not worry so, Canonchet. The most daring English raid could not find us now. There is not time, unless one of the English can call upon their god to show them the way." Stone-Wall smiled with contempt.

Canonchet smiled also, finding relief in Stone-Wall's words. Even the great God the English spoke of so often, he was sure, could never find his way through the great Swamp to the fortress.

"Still, hurry, my friend," Canonchet said, the left to check on the small contingent of warriors he had brought with him to the fort.

Indian Peter was no God, but he did know the way through the Swamp to the fort. And now that he was a captive of the English, he felt it best to lead them there so they could talk with his tribal leaders as they asked to, perhaps winning his own release.

He did not like being captive. He had heard other captives had been made slaves, put onto boats and taken off to far away lands. He wanted to stay here, on the water's edge he knew so well. The English had told him they wished to smooth over the ruffled feathers raised by the activities of Philip and his followers.

Indian Peter walked ahead of a long column of Englishmen, carefully picking out the muddy, soft trail leading to the fort. Beside him was the Englishman, Benjamin Church, and a man Church called "General."

"The Plymouth men have run out of provisions," Church complained. "How can men who call themselves soldiers be so damned shortsighted escapes my understanding."

"Colonel, where we're headed, provisions will be the least of our concern. Besides, we're only a day's march from the supply camp. Let the Plymouth stomachs grumble a bit. It'll harden them." General Winslow was in unusually good spirits. He was a man of action, and this expedition against the Narragansetts was all the action he could wish for.

"I'd feel better if the men had planned some."

"Are you suggesting we turn back, colonel? You, the advocate of chasing the enemy and fighting him wherever he is?" Winslow teased his driven subordinate.

"Nosir. I'm not saying any such thing. It's just a situation I thought you should be aware of."

"Well Colonel, I'm aware of it. Peter, how much farther do you figure?"

"Not too far. This path leads around that small bend," he said, pointing ahead of him about a hundred yards. "After that you catch glimpses of the walls, although it is still a few walks away."

"Very good. Colonel, see to it that the men have their guns loaded and ready with fresh powder."

"Yessir," Church said and stepped off the trail to wait for the main body of men to catch up.

"You have done well to lead us so far," Winslow said to his guide.

"Please sir, it is the least I can do for the consideration you have shown me, a captive," Indian Peter said in his most subservient manner. He did not want to be put on a boat.

"Impressive," Church whispered, looking through the trees at the stone walls of the fort. A few snowflakes fell. Church looked up, disgruntled. Above him dark clouds were gathering, threatening a December storm. Hardly time to be caught in the swamps, trying to besiege a fort.

"No use in waiting around," General Winslow said, also looking up at the sky. "When all the troops are up, we'll attack. Captain Gardner will lead the first assault. Church, you follow him inside. The rest of us will come in as we are able."

Within ten minutes Captain Gardner's troops stepped off. Now snow was falling heavily, covering the hats of the troopers with a fine, light powder.

"Careful to keep your powder dry, lads," Captain Gardner said as they stepped out into the clearing that led to the log.

Church and Winslow watched as long as they could, but the wind picked up and the snow was nothing less than a blizzard. By the time Gardner's men reached the gate they were lost to sight. But almost immediately Church heard the Indian warning cries sound and then gunfire, scattered at first, then increasing into an unbroken, continuous crackle.

"Church, lead your men forward and support Gardner," Winslow ordered. "I'll have the troops behind us lay a steady fire over the wall and into the fort for support."

Church yelled over the wind for his men to form up, then led them forward. Or at least he guessed he did. He could not see more than a few miserable feet ahead of him.

The sound of the battle grew louder. Gardner was running into stiff resistance, but as Church led his stumbling men forward the weather was their only obstacle. They carefully crossed the slippery log that led to the gate, waiting on the other side for a dozen men to cross before plunging through it.

Church's suspicion of stiff Indian resistance were confirmed. Several troopers lay dead in the gateway. Others cried out in wounded pain, but their cries were quickly lost in the howling wind.

"Trooper," Church addressed one man who was vainly trying to staunch the flow of blood from another man's chest with handfuls of snow. "Have you seen Captain Gardner?"

"Inside sir. We only broke through a minute ago." He turned his attention back to the fallen man. "Christ Johnny, I don't think there's much that can be done," he said, half to himself, half in explanation to his friend. Johnny just stared forward, eyes wide, alive but realizing life had only moments left in him. Church hurried inside the gate.

Confusion ruled inside. Gunfire was hotly exchanged, more even than Church had guessed from outside the wall. Inside the walls gave some protection from the wind, but the snow fell so quickly that the tracks of the men who preceded Church were lost to view. Now smoke started billowing, and Church could just detect the outline of burning wigwams. He coughed and his eyes watered, but he made out the figure of the man he sought.

"Captain Gardner!" he yelled through the haze, even though the man stood no more than ten feet in front of him. Gardner turned and saw him, stepped towards him, then fell. Church bent over him, lifting Gardner's cap and felt a small hole on his left temple, and a much larger one in the right rear of his head. Dropping the head back into the snow, Church twisted violently around trying to regain his bearings, then grabbed a trooper rushing past him, nearly pulling him to the ground.

"Yessir?" the man said, then glanced down at Gardner's face and grew wide-eyed. Church shook him hard to get his attention.

"Listen to me, trooper. Go back through the gate we just come in. Find General Winslow. Tell him to order his troops to stop firing. Got it?"

"Stop firing sir?" the trooper asked, bewildered.

"Yes, dammit. The troops outside the fort! Gardner caught one from outside, not in. We're shooting our own men. Now go!" He pushed the man forward toward the gate, quickly losing him in the swirl of smoke and snow. He found another man to care for Gardner who, despite the ball through his head, continued to wheeze and gasp for air.

The smoke turned even thicker. Horrible screams and cryings out could be heard through the gunfire, receding or becoming stupendously loud depending on the shifts of the wind. Church closed his eyes, bent forward with his gun, reopened his eyes, and plunged into the melee.

Canonchet stumbled through the smoke and snow, positioning his warriors to delay the oncoming English troops. Since the fort was a base of supply as well as a winter village, guns and ammunition were plentiful. What was not plentiful were warriors to use them. Old men, young boys, and even a few women joined the line and fired into the massed and confused English. But the sheer number of Englishmen meant they kept coming, burning wigwam after wigwam after wigwam as they did.

The fort - built to protect the village - was now their greatest enemy. With the English controlling the gate the villagers were squeezed between the English stomping down on them and the wall of their own design behind them. Canonchet had already assigned the biggest, strongest warriors to the point in the wall farthest away from the gate, and they busily worked with poles and iron bars, frantically tearing into the wall to make an avenue of escape for the village.

What might save the village was the weather, and the confusion it brought. But even the weather couldn't help those villagers who, fearing both the weather and the hail of English bullets, cowered deep inside their wigwams, refusing all pleas to come out. Canonchet was finally forced to leave them, and they'd either burn from the fires being set by the English, or be shot down as they ran, shrieking, from the huts which were alive with flame.

Canonchet went back to the place where the braves worked to create an escape. They'd managed to chop a small hole in the wall through which people squeezed one at a time. The warriors had also stacked the rubble in one pile next to the wall, where the more agile villagers could scramble up and over.

"Good," Canonchet yelled into the wind. "Round up everyone who will come and get them through it. I'm going back up to help with the defense."

He ran through the snow which combined with smoke to create a damp, icy, dirty sleet. He could tell he had reached the defensive line only from the increased sound of gunfire. It was no longer very far from the escape in the wall behind him.

Church searched desperately for General Winslow in the confusion. "Stop," he cried to a man about to put another wigwam to the torch. "Stop right now. There is no need!" The trooper looked at him quizzically, then touched the torch to the wigwam anyway, jumping back as its grass and twig construction crackled into flame. He stepped back and leveled his gun at the doorway, waiting for the flames to force anyone inside out.

Church, disgusted, searched on for Winslow. Stopping a single soldier wouldn't solve the problem. He staggered through the foot deep slush and finally found the General by the gate, calmly smoking his pipe.

"General, sir, you've got to order the men to stop torching the village. We have the enemy beaten. We can use the shelter for ourselves. And the food."

The General surveyed him calmly, taking a long draw on his pipe, then said, "Colonel, I'm not holing up in this godforsaken heathen village. I fully expect to return to our own base when this is over. Once we've finished here, we'll head back out on the trail."

"But sir, the men. . . ."

"Will want nothing more than to leave this mess behind them and make their way back to the safety of a town and garrison. Believe me, colonel, stay here and mutiny will be our concern. Now, if you please, take command outside the gate while I go inside and oversee the battle. There's reports the Indians have made a small escape in the rear of the fort, and other reports of a band of Indians approaching from the swamps."

Church stared at his commander in shock. Back on the trail? After a battle? During a blizzard? But orders were not to be questioned. He gathered himself up and marched off to lead the troops outside the fort. He passed Indian Peter, who sat on the ground, arms tightly wrapped around his knees, rocking back and forth, tears streaming down his eyes, mumbling and wailing. But Church did not notice him.

Canonchet, hearing that warriors had approached from outside, left the village wall and found them as they approached. There were thirty or forty of them.

"Form a line," he said, rushing them forward down the rail and spreading them out along a line at a right angle to the fortress wall, only a few dozen feet ahead of the breach. "Load your weapons and get ready to fire."

He peered into the storm, which had started to slacken. Out here the smoke didn't sting your eyes. Compared to the noise and blackness in the compound, the snow and wind seemed calm. A few more seconds and he vaguely made out the form of a trooper coming towards him, and behind him more troopers. He waited until the troopers were within a dozen feet of them, then yelled his command.

"Fire!"

The volley caught Church's men by surprise. Church himself felt the impact of two balls. One put a hole into his pocket, lodging in a heavy pair of mittens he had there, and did no harm. But the other cut into the fleshy part of his thigh and dark red blood oozed out the hole, the cold coagulating it as it did. But Church pressed forward, waving his cutlass and yelling encouragement to his men.

Indian resistance was stiff, and Church reckoned that they must have hit a force not originally in the village. He yelled to his men to hunker down and fight it out.

The battle continued for close to half an hour, neither side gaining the advantage it needed to drive off the other. But both were satisfied with this. For Church and his men it meant the fort could be completely destroyed. For Canonchet, it meant those that could escape were given the chance to do so.

Finally the last of the women and children that could be found were safely out and down the trail. Canonchet quickly planned a full retreat, hoping to slip away from the English fighters. He had warriors hold their fire for several minutes, until the English guns, uncertain of what had happened to cause this silence, also slackened their fire.

A few men started to slip forward from the English position. Canonchet let them come a few yards. Then a few more. Then his braves opened a furious fire on them, sending them scurrying back to their line. Now, as the English line again erupted in smoky battle, Canonchet ordered his men to prepare to retreat and, when the initial English volley was spent, the warriors slipped away into the depths of the swamp, knowing the English would think twice before daring to venture into the silence in front of them again.

Almost fifteen minutes of silence went by before Church and his men again crept forward and found the Indian position abandoned. Posting his men on watch, Church went back into the fort to find General Winslow.

The snow had stopped, although the sky threatened more. The wind had also died down, and smoke from hundreds of wigwam fires rose straight up into the gray sky. The ground was covered with a dirty, muddy slush, tinged with a deep red. Mixed into the slush were bodies, hundreds of them. Some were English. Most were Narragansett. Most of those were women and children. Some had been shot, others beaten. Still others had died from the lethal combination of smoke and flames. Those who had died early in the fight were half-covered by the snow, hulks that bore just a shadowy outline of a human form.

General Winslow stood in the middle of this, overseeing the systematic burning of those few wigwam storehouses that still remained. A bloodied rag wrapped around his head, only partly covered by a woolen cap, bore testament that his leadership had been active. Captain Mosely stood by him.

"Church," Winslow exclaimed happily as he saw the man approach. "A good day's work, eh?"

Church looked around him. It had indeed been a good day's work, although Church found it hard to think of it that way. A hard blow had been struck against the Narragansett, just as the leaders of the colonies had hoped. Their winter fortress was destroyed, along with their winter stores of grain and food. It would be a long, hard winter for the Narragansett, perhaps a devastating one. But war, no matter how just, was still a grim business.

"General, I still say we should camp here for the night. Use those wigwams as shelter. Use the food to replenish ourselves. Look at the wounded," Church said, pointing to where five dozen men lay in various states of carnage. "How are we going to move them back to Wickford without killing half of them?"

Winslow listened to his argument, but Captain Mosely quickly countered him. "By Gosh, I've fought these red savages before. We done a good day's work here, general, but we ain't even begun to touch the main bunch of savages. You can bet they're on their way here now, madder then hell. And they ain't had a foodless winter to take the starch out of them yet. We stay here General, it's not just the badly wounded that'll die, it's the whole damn troop."

Winslow kicked at the snow, pondering his course. He looked up and saw the company's surgeon tending the wounded and called him over.

"Should we stay, or head back to Wickford? From a medicinal point of view."

The doctor, unsure how to answer, looked around the blackened, smoky village, then turned back to the General. "Frankly sir, the march back is going to be rough on them. But I don't see what staying here is going to gain us. It'll just be that much longer before I can care for them proper."

"That's it then. We go," the general declared.

"But General," Church protested, "One night is all I say. Let the storm pass. Let the men sleep, and fill their stomachs. . . "

"No Church. The decision's made. Besides, seems the worst of the storm is passed. Mosely, oversee the burning of the remaining huts. Church, you. . . Church?"

Church wavered back and forth, then staggered forward and fell to the ground. He rolled over onto his back and reached down to his thigh, caked with blood and dirt.

"Doctor," Winslow called to the medical man who was making his way back to the mass of wounded. "Another patient for you over here."

The main group of Narragansetts did not arrive in time to pursue the straggly column of English as it made its way over the thin, snowy trail back to Wickford. Nor could Canonchet spare enough men to harass the column. Hundreds of now homeless villagers had to be provided for. Dozens more were wounded and dying.

He did send a few scouts to watch the procession, and they brought back stories of death and despair, of bodies left along the trail as the wounded died. The scouts counted almost fifty.

But the suffering the English were enduring could never come close to balancing the suffering of the Narragansett. As Canonchet oversaw the setting up of a temporary camp and the salvaging of what food stores could be taken away, an overpowering resolve grabbed hold with a fierceness that Canonchet knew wouldn't die, even in the rugged winter that lay ahead.

The English must pay for this outrage, for this attack on women and children, for this cowardly act that they would try to explain away as a necessary part of war.

And he would see that the English would pay. And not just with a few cattle, or a few lives. Canonchet resolved that the English would be driven into the sea.

Thousand of warriors flocked to the Menamaset camp. Most were Narragansetts under Canonchet, but dozens more came in daily, drawn by the knowledge of war in the spring, a war now being fought not only by my small, brave band of men, but by the mighty Narragansett under the leadership of the famed warrior, Canonchet.

When I had first straggled back to Menamaset, accompanied by less than two dozen of my four hundred warriors, my fortunes appeared bleak. Others straggled in over the next few weeks, but in all less than forty came back from the Mohawk defeat. Charles was among the missing.

Matoonas welcomed me back with open arms and ceremony. Muttawmp also joined in, although grudgingly. Muttawmp thought my defeat at the hands of the Mohawks clearly showed how unfit for leadership I was, especially when compared to the string of successes he himself had planned and led.

But Muttawmp also saw that, no matter what his own feelings, most of the warriors streaming into camp came to fight under King Philip, the rebel leader the English so feared. So Muttawmp reluctantly joined with Matoonas in the ceremonies honoring me.

On my arrival the news had not been good. Along with my own disaster, rumors of a major defeat of the Narragansett crept into camp. For a while very few men came to join them. Many went home.

My mood had been no better. My defeat shook my own resolve. Who was I to lead my nation into what could be a final war? Had I begun all this only to see my own Wampanoags killed, not by the English, but by a rival Indian nation?

But the immediate demands for leadership pushed down my feelings of self doubt. A few days of unrelenting organizing, cajoling, and handling the inevitable disputes that arose between the many sachems and tribes first tempered my despair. A few more days of it, and I began to feel a revival of my spirit. Soon I knew that, despite my own setback, the war must be pressed forward vigorously.

And as the story of the Great Swamp Fight became known, and the main army of the Narragansetts headed north, outrage at the English act combined with the knowledge that the great fighting strength of the Narragansett was left virtually intact to create a new sense of hope.

Since the coming of Canonchet, the sachems had been too busy gathering and organizing the stuff of every day life to plan the spring campaign. Food and shelter had to be found, transported, distributed, then found again. New arrivals usually came with no more than a few days' food, although most had some form of tents and skins. The Narragansett, however, had to be provided for nearly from scratch, as much of their stores and belongings had been destroyed in the Great Swamp.

It was a huge effort, and I found myself at the center of it, as Wootonekanuske discovered when she rejoined me in early February. She found me organizing a dozen warriors for a hunting trip to the North country, in hopes of finding game there, since most of the game in the surrounding forests had been used up long before. Wootonekanuske had left me there to finish, searching out the small shelter made of stretched skins over sticks that served as my home - a far cry from the sturdy winter wigwams we'd shared in years past.

By the time I joined my wife and son she had put together a broth made from fish heads and boiled chestnuts, as well as a bit of corn mash.

"You look tired," she noted as I came in.

I smiled. "When have you known me not to be so?" I asked. Then, while she turned to the stew I talked quietly with my son, asking about the trip from the south where they had dwelt with Weetamoo while I had been west. I lazily scratched Three Toes, who had come with them and who, after a boisterous greeting, now settled at my feet.

The stew served, Wootonekanuske once again settled back to study me, after suggesting to our son to go out and find his friends.

"I hear you are like the wind, everywhere at once, moving all things," she said.

"I do what I must. I do what I can. It is not easy. Too many sachems who feel they know best what should be done."

"And you must lead them?"

"Hardly. If I were to try to lead them, they would purposefully go the opposite way. They are proud men, even the least of them. They must be persuaded."

"And so you persuade them."

"I try. So do others. But most do not know more than a few of the others. Even Canonchet, so well known by name, is only recognized by a dozen. My years of travel have made me familiar with the greater number of them. Since I know them, I can speak to them more easily. 'Persuade' them."

"You are the leader then," Wootonekanuske said. "Even if they do not acknowledge it."

I did not counter her. While others would shrink from naming me as such, I did indeed feel I was still the force behind the war, that it was my spirit that moved the warriors. But it was a thought I dared not speak, even to myself.

"So many warriors," Wootonekanuske observed. "Many men to do the fighting. There will be battles in the spring?"

"That is certain. But we have not yet started to plan them. It has been job enough just feeding them all. Still, before long the weather will warm. Plans

must be made for the spring. We cannot allow the English to get ahead of us. We must attack them before they expect it. That is why I have asked for a meeting of the major sachems for tomorrow night. To begin planning. To decide what will be done."

"Tomorrow night? What of tonight then?" She moved closer to me, and I felt the pleasant warmth of her body on mine.

"Tonight?" I said, feeling the worries of the last few months melt away. "Tonight I must reacquaint myself with my wife." I slid my arm around her waist.

"Metacomet speaks wisely," Matoonas said to the gathered sachems. "Soon spring will be upon us, and so will the English. We must plan now and make the English the hunted, instead of the hunter."

"With that there can be no disagreement," said Canonchet from his seat near the council fire, across from Matoonas and me. Next to Canonchet sat Muttawmp. "To wait for the English to attack is to give him the advantage. We must not let them set the terms of the war."

"That is why we must bring down our blow first," I said. "And it must be aimed at the very heart of the enemy. We must gather our forces into a single, massed army that will strike at the very center of the English. We must drive directly into the enemy with all the force we have. We must deliver a hammer blow which will shock them and destroy them."

There was a moment of quiet, a moment where I held my breath, hoping my point had carried.

"And where should this blow be delivered?" Muttawmp asked quietly.

"Boston!" I said it hard, and with conviction.

There was a murmuring through the sachems gathered around the fire. Boston? The very core of English strength? How could it even be considered?

Muttawmp was the first to give voice to these doubts.

"Strong words, Metacomet. But how do you propose we attack Boston by surprise? Would we not first have to go through towns that lie outside it? And if we do, will that not give them time to fortify?" The murmuring rose again, most agreeing with the concerns of Muttawmp, but quieted as they turned to hear my answer.

"Of course they will hurry to the defensive. That is why several towns must be attacked at the same time. But most will be raids, designed to confuse the English and throw them off. We have seen from the fall campaign that wherever we attack, a force is sent out to meet us. I propose a series of small attacks along the outer ring of Boston towns, which will again be met with troops sent out from Boston. Once they are dispersed, our main force will deliver the hard blow from the opposite direction of the small raids. That force will find virtually no

resistance to their march, and before the English realize what they are facing, we will be upon their backs. Victory will be ours."

"Victory over the Massachusetts men," Muttawmp agreed, "But what of Plymouth, and Connecticut? Will they not bring their forces to bear?"

"Of course. But without the strength of Massachusetts, our victorious forces will be able to meet them strength for strength, and defeat them. If we look to destroy the English, this is how it must be done. With a strong, mighty blow that will defeat the Massachusetts men, and demoralize the rest. Then they will get on their ships and head back across the sea from which they came, happy to still have their lives."

I sat back and enjoyed the silence that surrounded me. The gathered sachems were astounded. Awed by it. Its very brazenness attracted them. Its lofty ambition gave it an air of invincibility. How could they lose with such a plan?

Even Muttawmp, who clearly did not like it, or at least did not like the fact that I had been the one to propose it, looked around the council fire, gauging reaction, trying to see if there was a chance to oppose it. But this very searching lessened his position. By asking the eyes of other sachems for support, they refused it to him. They would not oppose the plan of the renowned King Philip. Sachems who thought themselves mighty now saw themselves in a very different light when comparing themselves to my plan of battle.

Except Canonchet. He did not make Muttawmp's mistake of searching for silent support. He knew he had the respect of his warriors, and that was all he needed. He waited for the silence to settle in, then just before I was about to speak again, he spoke instead.

"I would like to suggest another plan," he said simply, but with a deep, resonant authority that commanded more respect than his simple words. All fell quiet, including me.

"As you know, I have led my warriors through many battles, and many wars. Some of you here have felt the might of my men against your villages." He looked around now, not in search of support, but to confirm this fact, which many nodded to, with memories they would rather forget.

"But that is all in the past. Philip speaks the truth. Today the only enemy of the Narragansett is the white man. All others are our friends and allies. It must be so.

"As for the coming spring, the plan proposed by Metacomet is a good and worthy one, one that deserves our careful consideration. But I too have thought about the offensive and what must be done. I have thought of one truth which forms the basis for my plan, and I ask that it also be given the courtesy of consideration. It is easier to attack an enemy where he is not ready than where he is."

Murmuring agreement spread around the council fire. I sensed that Canonchet was leading us down a path I did not want to go, and I risked interruption.

"That is true, my friend. It is always easier, but the easiest way is not always the way that achieves the most. We are after achievement."

Canonchet showed no irritation at the interruption. "Agreed. It is achievement we are after. And what is it we want to achieve? You have said it yourself, Metacomet. We want the Englishmen gone from our shores. But how is this to be achieved? By defeating their armies? Perhaps. But defeat of their armies does not drive them from their homes. Often, it only makes them replenish their army and fight all the more.

"No. What must be done is clear. We must drive the white men from their homes as they have driven us from ours." His reference to the fight at the Great Swamp was not lost on those around the fire.

"And where are those homes?" Canonchet continued. "They are spread out all through our lands, Each a separate, growing community. As weeds in a garden they continue to sprout anew, dependent on little but themselves. It is these that must be our target. The English army's strength lies in its numbers and its weapons. Our strength is in our cunning, and our speed. Let us use our strengths to defeat their strengths. The white man has given us a hundred targets. Why strike at the one that is the most protected, hoping to trick the enemy into allowing it? Strike instead at one left unprotected. Destroy it. Then destroy the next, and the next. And when the army leaves the one it protects, strike that one. Soon their army will have nothing left to protect. Only then shall we see the last of the white man."

The sachems started talking amongst themselves, arguing the merits of the two plans they had heard. I tried to hear what the sachems were saying, tried to gauge their sentiment, but only heard many voices arguing many sides. I whispered into the ear of Matoonas, who nodded, then rose, asking for the attention of the sachems. I leaned back, looking into the faces of the sachems to read their thoughts of the words Matoonas was about to speak.

"Noble Canonchet, your words are strong, and your tactics sound. But still, I must ask a question, if only to clear up my own fogginess of thinking. How long would this campaign take?"

Canonchet allowed no hesitation in his answer. "As long as it must. As long as the Englishmen are on our shores."

"Have you a plan to supply our warriors for that time? Metacomet's plan has with it the advantage of speed, of a forced blow to the enemy that would not strain our food and hunting, and subject our people to the starvation of war."

To the gathered sachems, Matoonas' concern was all too real. All of them had faced lean, hungry winters, even in times of relative peace. War always made these problems worse.

But again Canonchet let no time pass for those thoughts to take root.

"It is a matter I have given much thought too. I can tell you what must be done. We have thousands of warriors gathered. But we also have thousands who are not warriors. Those people must be organized into an army as well. They must be brought to the most fertile of our fields, well away from the English enemy. There they will work together to farm and harvest. Much have we learned from the English about planting, and all this must be put to use there.

"Our best hunters will be sent out to help to bring in more food. Their help in this manner will be as valuable to us as any warrior.

"Lastly, our own attacks upon the village of the white man will bring us more supplies. Every town has in it abundant supplies of grains and cattle. These we will turn to our own use. We will attack those towns first that are a center of food for the English. Boston itself relies on the food grown elsewhere for survival. Cut off Boston's food, and attacking it will become unnecessary. It will wither away like a vine with no roots."

Matoonas looked to me, and I gestured that he should resume his seat. The fire was quiet as the sachems looked first from Canonchet, then to me, then back again, waiting to see if either of us would back down. If neither did, then what?

I reviewed the situation in his mind. Canonchet had thrown down the challenge. He wanted military leadership of the war, something I felt was rightfully mine. I found it hard to resist challenging Canonchet then and there, feeling most would follow me. But would Canonchet? And if not, would those he led? I needed more time to approach the Narragansett sachems individually, using my own persuasive force in face to face encounters.

But I also needed to reestablish my leadership, however nominal, at the council fire. I stood.

"Great Canonchet, your words are welcome. What lies before us is a large task, and one that cannot be decided rashly. We now have had the benefit of our collected thoughts and wisdom. For now that is enough. I say we consider the words spoken here tonight, and return to the council fire in seven days time. Then the decision shall be made."

I looked to Canonchet to see if there was objection, but Canonchet's face betrayed no thoughts one way or the other, I left no time for him to change this attitude. I walked through the ring around the council fire, followed by Matoonas and several other sachems. The meeting was over.

Matoonas could scarcely contain his fury until we were out of hearing of the others, then he exploded in whispered exclamations.

"Who is Canonchet that he should grab hold of all we have done so far? Where was he in those years when you went from camp to camp, warning us of the very dangers we now face? Where was he when we fought the English at Brookfield, and at Springfield? Sitting on his rump, telling the English they need

not be concerned by him! And now he comes to our council fire and presumes to tell us how the battle will be won."

I could not help but smile at the outrage exhibited by my friend, even though it echoed my own. And in its echo I could find my own calm.

"Do not forget, Matoonas, it was we who begged Canonchet to join our council fire. He cannot be faulted for wishing to do so on his own terms. Besides, he is a great warrior. I must think out for myself whether his way may not be the better one. But come, we have work to do, and seven days in which to do it. We must talk with the leaders of the tribes, find out their thoughts. Our work must be done carefully. We must not antagonize, for we will need them all. But we must convince them."

"And what shall we convince them of?" Matoonas asked.

"The truth of what you just finished explaining to me."

For the next seven days I felt as if the last fourteen years had been pushed into one small basket. Sachems I had spoken to dozens of times I spoke to again now. Tribe members under the sachems who had in the past been friendly to my arguments I enlisted anew in my push to ensure the proper outcome at the next council fire.

I had carefully thought through Canonchet's plan, and still felt it weaker than my own. Canonchet, I argued again and again, offered it only to preserve his own claim to leadership of the emerging Algonquin nation. Canonchet is too ambitious, I unashamedly whispered in the ears of those I wanted to persuade.

Around the tribal fires I went to my arguments won new friends among those who had come to listen. But the same was not true at the tribal fires I could not attend.

Matoonas attended as many councils as me, arguing for our position. "At every fire, you have supporters," he told me, "But they do not carry the day. The older members of the tribe say that you are a great speaker, but that Canonchet is the greater warrior. And this is now war, they say. They compare your defeat by the Mohawks to Canonchet's reputation for generalship."

"But my plan? Do they see the advantages of my plan?" I asked.

Matoonas shook his head. "They see safety in Canonchet's plan. They see a chance to pull back and negotiate should things go badly. They say your plan risks everything. It risks the very existence of the Algonquin. Canonchet's, they say, may or may not be more successful than your own, but it will never be the disaster yours could prove to be. Canonchet's followers spread horrible stories of the fate that awaits our villages should our army, driving into the heart of the enemy, be cut off and destroyed, with nothing left for the defense.

"The younger ones support you, Metacomet. It is the older ones who speak this way. They will oppose you as long as Canonchet does."

I had to shake my head in agreement. I had seen the minds of sachem change under my own arguments, but I knew that without my own presence, my own character there to press the arguments, Canonchet's plan would win out.

"Tell the others to stop arguing at the tribal fires," I instructed Matoonas.

"You are giving up?" he asked in disbelief.

"No, not giving up," I replied. "But the situation calls for a change in tactics. I will speak with one more sachem. Then we shall see."

"Canonchet, may I speak with you privately?"

Canonchet waved away the warriors seated by him and bid me sit next to him on a brightly colored blanket. I did so, my legs knotted in front of me. Canonchet wordlessly offered me a pipe. I took it readily, and let the bitter smoke fill my lungs. I held onto it, feeling its heat in my chest for several moments before expelling the smoke through my nostrils.

"I have come to speak to you privately about the military matters that face us. If we have disagreements, let us work them out here, between us, and not raise further dissension among the tribe. Our path is long enough without filling it with extra logs to climb over."

"You have no disagreement here," Canonchet said, but then waited for me to continue.

"I have thought through the plan you presented, Canonchet, and still do not feel it is as strong as my own. I have heard your argument. My plan, you say, risks everything. Defeat would mean the destruction of our nation. But I must ask you this, do you think if we suffer defeat with your plan, the final result will be any different?"

"Yes. Because with my plan, we will never be defeated. We may not push them into the sea. We may not destroy the English. But wherever we take them on, we will defeat them. That alone will assure our future."

"Our future cannot be assured as long as the English are present. Already they outnumber us, and they have been here but fifty years. Every year brings more ships filled with more English. If they are not stopped, they cannot help but overwhelm us. Surely you see that?"

"I see that all too well, Metacomet. It is another reason I do not agree with your plan. We will be overwhelmed."

"Then we must risk all." I insisted.

"Risk, I agree. But a straight forward attack, no matter how well planned, is not risk. It is sacrifice. It is suicide. I cannot agree to it."

I took another lungful of smoke from the pipe. I was still sure of my plan, and still felt Canonchet's resistance to it was based more on pride than military considerations. I saw only one hope left.

"Canonchet, I believe my plan to be the right one - the one that can bring victory. But I also believe it needs our greatest warrior to bring it about. That is why I would propose at the meeting that, if my plan is adopted, you would be its commander. You would lead the forces into battle."

Now it was Canonchet's turn to take a long, slow draw of his pipe. He held the smoke in his lungs for a full minute before letting it slip slowly from his lips. He turned his long, solemn face towards me, and I saw for the first time an earnest intensity burning in Canonchet's eyes.

"I do not think the English can be driven from our land, Metacomet. But I do believe you're right to say our people must come together. And they are, thanks

in large part to the work you have done these many years. But to cement them together, to make them truly one nation, we must win victories. Through victory, a strength will be forged, a strength the English will respect. Remember this, our recent victories over the English have shown us we can defeat them in battle. But it has also done something I think more important. It has shown the English they can lose. And a well planned series of attacks in the spring will reinforce this. If they are never countered by the English we may yet fulfill your dream of driving them into the sea. But even if we cannot continue after a time, our victories will teach the English they can no longer treat us with the contempt they have shown in the last years.

"If I believed in your plan, my friend, I would want you to lead it, because a leader must believe in where he takes his people. If I am to lead, then I must lead them the way I have shown. Otherwise only bad can come of it."

"If the Council decides my plan is the better one, will you follow me?" I asked.

"I will not lead my people down a path I do not believe in."

Silence fell between us. We both took long puffs on the ornately carved pipe. I rose to leave, but as I did Canonchet spoke again.

"I believe in the need for unity between our people, Metacomet. And it is you who convinced me of that. But I will not stand by and watch our new strength wasted in a foolish attack. I hope you will not choose to lead us that way."

I walked silently away.

I did not speak to Matoonas after I had talked with Canonchet, and Matoonas did not press me, even though I knew he longed to hear what had taken place. It agitated him. He knew me as one who only let silences last as long as it took me to form my next argument. And that was in fact what I was now doing, although now it meant being silent for two days.

Canonchet too remained quiet, and instructed his men not to argue at the tribal fires. The arguments themselves continued, but were debates among the tribal members themselves, although at many fires the sudden silence of the more well known sachems, and the unknown reasons for that silence, was often the subject of the most intense discussions.

But tribal discussions were soon over, as once again the sachems gathered to discuss the spring campaign.

As the sachems arranged themselves, I waited out of their sight. Only when they were all seated with the fire burning brightly did I arrive, a few moments after Canonchet. We arrived only seconds apart, but we were clearly not yet together.

The sachems fell silent. Only when it became clear that neither Canonchet nor myself were going to speak did Muttawmp, acting as host in his own territory, take it upon himself to begin.

"It is time again to consider our spring campaign, and what strategy we will use against the Englishmen. I will state plainly, I favor the strategy that attacks the enemy at their weakest, but we must be sure our attacks never hesitate for want of a target. As we attack the weaker settlements, it must only be a prelude to attacking the stronger. In this way they will learn to fear our attack, and we will gain strength, both spiritually and from the word of our victories."

Matoonas cleared his throat and, in recognition of his association with me, the sachems turned their attention to him, trying to learn my position through him.

"I must disagree with my honored friend. Trying to destroy the white man by attacking his villages will be like trying to destroy a beehive by stepping on each bee. Only when the hive is attacked and destroyed will the bees be driven away."

The ice broken, the sides drawn, individual sachems now spoke their thoughts, one after the other, and I listened as each, emboldened by the one who spoke before, gave their views. It was a close thing, but those favoring Canonchet's way outnumbered those who favored mine. Most importantly, those I knew neither to favor myself or Canonchet personally tended to side with Canonchet. The clear sentiment then was that Canonchet's plan was the better one. Those who argued for mine did so out of loyalty to me, a loyalty I appreciated deeply, but whose limits had been tested, and it was time to bring all together.

"Friends," I said, my voice cutting off a young sachem from a northern tribe. The sachem fell silent, ceding the fire to me. "It does us no good to bicker any further. We must be united in war. I now agree the best plan is the one presented to us by Canonchet. I am prepared to follow Canonchet into battle, as I hope all of you will also do."

There was a heavy silence after I stopped speaking. Matoonas looked searchingly at me, but I willed my features to remain impassive. With my continuing silence, eyes moved from me to Canonchet who, after a slightly longer pause, spoke.

"I am honored that such a great leader as Metacomet would follow me into battle. But I will not allow it," he said, and there was a silent gasp in the crowd. "How can one follow another who is by my side? There is no room for a single leader. We must all be leaders in the war to come."

Canonchet's eloquent words were welcomed with pleasure by all the sachems. A general hubbub arose as each turned to the next in new harmony. Surely if Canonchet and Philip could put aside their difference so could they. But Canonchet did not let the talking go on long before asserting his generalship.

"Come, we must plan. There is much to do before the spring thaws."

During the next weeks my presence was greeted with respect wherever I went. But as preparations went on I became increasingly restless, feeling the battle preparations were Canonchet's, not mine.

Instead I devoted my time and efforts to the almost overwhelming supply problems facing the warriors, gathering weapons and food into the camps, and making preparations for supplies throughout the year as Canonchet's plan required. Supplies would be the life or death of the campaign.

I oversaw the establishment of a large supply camp at Peskeompskut, near the abandoned English town of Deerfield, putting hundreds of women and older men to work preparing the fields, and setting up wigwams where the plentiful fish caught in the nearby Connecticut River would be dried out and stored for the winter months. It was a huge task, requiring my nearly ceaseless attention. And yet I couldn't help but feel I was playing only a minor role in the coming war. I was a supply master, instead of a leader of warriors. But my attempts at influencing strategy were politely rebuffed by Canonchet, despite his talk about us all being leaders.

"All give me respect, and listen to the ideas I have," I complained to Wootonekanuske one sunny afternoon, a day that was the leading edge to spring. "But they are never followed through with, unless I stand over them."

Wootonekanuske looked at me with sympathy. She'd seen me in many moods over the year, sad, mad, even elated. But I knew she'd never seen me this way before. Frustrated and left out.

"Do not worry, my husband," she soothed. The spring is fresh. The war is new. It will not be long before the battles begin. When they do, those with true leadership will be called on. Your time will come, I am sure of it."

I looked at my wife, her proud smile warming my soul, and could not help but return it. I reached out my hand and, as she had done so many times in the past, she took it in hers, her touch renewing my own confidence in myself.

Lancaster - February 10, 1676

Even now, leading a column of four hundred warriors from a dozen different tribes towards their first major battle with the English, even among his own Nashaway tribe, he was still better known by his English name - One-eyed John.

But while his name might sound undistinguished, he was far from it. His fame as a leader in battle had spread throughout the Algonquin nation. He, Monoco, had been chosen by Canonchet and Muttawmp to lead this first battle, the one that would set the stage for the war to come. It had been planned by Canonchet and Muttawmp. But it was Monoco who would see that it was carried out to the fullest measure.

There were signs the English knew he was coming. A few braves, never fully trusted, were missing from the camp, and those who knew them suspected they were providing information to the English. But the decision had been made to go forward and now, in the cover of the darkness, the warriors under Monoco's command approached Lancaster and its sixty families.

He had attacked it once before, in the early days of the conflict, when news of Philip's attacks had first fired his imagination. He had burned a house, killed a half-dozen villagers. But he had commanded only a few dozen warriors, and the small attack was the most he could mount.

Tonight was different. Knowing the layout of the town, he had sent warriors to destroy the bridge on the trail leading from Concord to this outlying community. This would not only prevent attack from Concord, but also retreat from Lancaster. No longer was the purpose of an attack a stinging raid. This attack was meant to destroy.

Dawn approached, figures became slight shadows in the awakening light. Monoco personally and skillfully arrayed his forces, surrounding the town, and hiding small bands of men where they could strike after the main thrust had hit the defenders, furthering their confusion and thwarting any counterattacks.

His forces in place, Monoco again surveyed the neatly laid out village with its solid, snug homes surrounded by barns and fields still covered with a soft layer of snow. As the sun's orange rim came up over the hills in front of them a few chimneys began to pour out heavier smoke, a sign that some of the villagers were starting to rise.

It was time.

He signaled the two hundred warriors he'd saved for the main attack, and they followed him across the field, slowly at first, then faster and faster as the yards passed beneath them and the houses drew nearer and nearer. With only a hundred yards left they broke into a run and, seeing a door open and a man step outside and catch sight of the onrushing host, Monoco let out a piercing, high pitched shriek, quickly taken up by the others around him.

Shots were fired, but the man quickly disappeared behind a closed door. Others, alerted by the screams they heard, came to their doors and windows. One, throwing his door wide open behind him, ran down the main road through the village.

"Indian attack! Indians! The Indians are attacking! Rise. . ."

A volley of musket fire drowned out his words, and he crumpled down into the snow, his blood soaking it red around him.

The Indians reached the outermost homes, firing tremendous volleys of musket balls into houses. One, maybe two shots were returned before the inhabitants were either shot down, or dragged out into the snow in their nightclothes. Excited shrieks mixed with terrified screams as the clothes of the helpless villagers were stripped from their bodies and tomahawks brought down into their heads.

One man, naked, bloody from a tomahawk blow that hadn't hit true, his skull split above his left ear, crawled on his hands and knees, blinded by the flow of blood, calling "Anna, Anna!" A warrior, whether out of hate or mercy, pulled his head up by the hair and slit his throat.

In a few minutes the first attack wave was over. Those villagers not already killed had retreated into six garrison houses, each surrounded by dozens of Indians.

While a lively, if sparse, musket fire kept the garrisons busy, Monoco had other Indians systematically burn the remaining three dozen houses, then turn to the public buildings such as the schoolhouse and church. As each burned, it added its own black smoke to the rising murky darkness of the others, creating a sinister plume in the bright February sky that was visible for miles.

Other warriors were given the task of driving off cattle. Still others were sent to make sure the village grain and seed supply was dumped and trodden into the snowy mud, thereby made useless. All that would be left were charred, smoky ruins in place of what had been only a few hours before a prosperous village.

The town razed, Monoco now turned his attention to the garrison houses. While not as crucial as the destruction of the town, he wanted to finish the job he had started. Like a weed in an herb garden, the English could only be gotten rid of by striking out every last root.

He chose the garrison farthest from him to attack first. Because of its position, attackers were not subject to crossfire from the other garrisons. It was built on a sloping hillside, and Monoco sent a large group to the top of the hill. There they could fire down at the house in safety while their shots found their marks accurately and deadly whenever a defender showed his face at a cutout. Screams of pain were heard as first one defender, than another, were hit by the steady rain of lead that showered into the stout log home.

But as the morning dragged on, Monoco could see firepower alone would not bring down the fortress. Logs were too good a stop for the heavy musket balls. As long as the defenders didn't show themselves, and they weren't now, they remained safe.

Monoco studied the garrison house, and his eyes rested on the ample supply of firewood stacked up against the rear portion of the house. The firewood provided both a defense against winter's cold, and against the rain of lead that was coming down from the hillside.

Monoco made his way to a barn nearby, where his Indian warriors were methodically stacking straw and sticks, preparing to burn it down. Monoco pointed to a large, two wheeled, wooden cart sitting empty in the corner.

"Fill that with hay and rope and bring it outside," he said. The warriors obeyed without question. He went outside to wait.

It was ready in a few minutes.

"Light it on fire," he commanded. A young warrior stepped to the cart and, pulling flint from his pouch, had a small flame started in a few moments. A few more minutes and a steady flame burned in the hay overflowing the edges of the cart.

Monoco watched with satisfaction. "Now," he said, "Two of you push the cart to that woodpile next to the garrison."

Without hesitation two young braves, anxious to impress their leader with their courage, grabbed hold of the cart handles and, using it as a shield against the few bullets that came from the garrison house, pushed it into the woodpile at the side of the house, retreating without injury.

For a few minutes the flames crackled and sputtered as they spread their deadly flame in the cart's hay. The warriors watched the flame grow, momentarily halting their gunfire, although the musket fire still being exchanged at the other garrison houses kept up the steady din.

Suddenly a figure emerged from the garrison house, bucket in hand, and with a few quick steps, emptied its contents onto the still spreading flames, ending them.

A hail of gunfire erupted, but the man scurried safely back into the garrison.

Almost immediately the warrior that had first lit the cart sprang back to its side. Standing next to the cart he was able to shield himself from the gunfire showering down from the garrison. After finding and gathering several handfuls of dry straw, he struck his flint and relit the flame. Only after assuring himself the fire was well started did he break away back to the safety of the others.

But as he did, a ball nearly found its mark, passing through the fleshy part of his calf, sending him to the ground in agony. Scared for his life he fought to regain his feet and stumbled the last few steps to safety before collapsing in the arms of one of his fellow braves. His chest heaving, he opened his eyes to see the smile of his sachem look down on him.

"Good work," Monoco said to the young man, who smiled back before wincing as the pain from his leg again shot through him. Monoco turned his gaze back to the cart, now bright with fire.

This time the steady gunfire from the warriors on the hill kept away any of those inside who might have had further ideas of smothering the flames. In ten minutes the cart was fully ablaze, setting the pile of logs next to it on fire as well, as Monoco had hoped. A few more minutes and flames crept up the side of the garrison house, and then onto the roof.

Black smoke erupted from the upper story windows. Another twenty minutes and the lower windows showed wisps of smoke. The timber that made up the roof supports creaked and moaned, threatening to give way as the flame soaked their strength out of them.

The front door of the garrison flew open, and a throng of people, men, women and children, came pouring out, the men stopping to kneel and fire, hoping to cover for the others as they made a desperate rush for the next garrison house.

But the Indians were ready. They ducked below the volley and, before the men could reload, rushed the forty villagers, surrounding them and cutting off their route to the next garrison house.

The men and older boys were killed, one after the other, with gunshots or tomahawk blows. The women and children were dragged off back towards the path the Indians had come. When it was over a dozen men lay dead in the small area in front of the garrison house. Two dozen women and children were force-marched along the trails back to the main camp, several miles distant.

With the battle for the first garrison house over, Monoco turned his attention to the next, again ordering a steady rain of gunshot a the wooded fortress, drowning out the anguished cries that came from those inside who had witnessed the killing and hauling away of their neighbors.

But before the second attack was fully underway, a scout came to Monoco, warning that a troop of forty English had forded the river and were on their way to relieve the garrisons. He briefly considered forming a line to fight them, but quickly reconsidered. It had been the decision of the council not to engage the armies of the enemy when no gain could result. A quick sweep of the village showed the attack's purpose had been fulfilled. Lancaster was a smoky ruin. Despite the remaining garrisons, it would have to be abandoned.

Keeping up a steady fire on those garrisons, Monoco ordered his other forces away from the village and began an orderly retreat of the remaining men. He himself was the last to leave.

When the mounted troopers arrived, no Indians were in sight. A hundred villagers wandered numbly out of the five remaining garrison houses. Three babies clutched tightly in their mothers' arms cried. All around were the blackened ruins and charred and bloody bodies of the inhabitants of Lancaster.

"Who led the attack?" asked Captain Wadsworth, head of the relief column.

One of the weary men, face blackened from the constant fire of muskets throughout the long morning, looked up, the whites of his eyes forming a ghostly silhouette.

"It was Philip," he said slowly, but firmly "The savage devil himself - King Philip."

Medfield - February, 1676

Samuel Morse crept carefully out of bed so as not to disturb his wife. It was still dark outside, but Samuel was always an early riser. He pulled on his pants, then the rough, worn, leather boots he wore on these cold mornings. He threw a coarse, heavy shirt over his nightshirt and strode out to the barn in the receding darkness.

The barn was still dark, even as the sun rose in the eastern sky. Samuel patted the rear end of the cow nearest him.

"Hungry this morning?" he asked the cow, then stroked its neck absentmindedly for a few moments before going into the shed room for hay.

A movement in the hay caught his eye. At first he suspected it was a rat, but then realized it was far too big. The news of the events a few days before Lancaster fresh in his mind, he had no doubts about what it was. He thought of his gun, loaded in readiness near the door of the house. If only he'd brought it with him. But what if he had? Kill one, and there'd probably be a hundred down on him and his family before you could reload, or escape.

The fact that the Indian hadn't leapt out convinced Samuel that the Indian thought he was undetected. Samuel decided it was best to let him believe that. Grabbing the nearest bunch of hay, he turned back into the barn.

Once inside he lost no time pushing his cattle outside. They'd stand a better chance of survival loose than trapped in a barn that could well be a pile of cinders in a few hours. Then he quickly retraced his steps into the house.

He shook his wife, signaling to her to be quiet even as her eyes opened to see his face.

"Indians," he whispered. "Outside. Get the children, but keep quiet. We've got to get to the garrison."

Instantly alert, his wife rose and threw a coat on over her nightclothes, then roused the sleepy children out of the loft. Samuel gathered his gun, powder keg, and the leather bag full of bullets, many molded by candlelight in the last few evenings after the news of Lancaster had reached them.

They gathered near the doorway, and when all were accounted for, Samuel slowly opened the front door. Darkness had given way to the eerie light and stillness of the pre-dawn. They hurried down the first three hundred feet of Main Street, eyes firmly on the garrison house still a hundred feet ahead. Behind them a loud shriek sounded, obviously a cry of alarm as one of the Indians scouts realized they'd been discovered.

"Run!" Samuel commanded, and the family broke into a frantic race as Indians shrieked all around them. Samuel didn't stop to see where they were or to shoot. His best chances of survival, for him and his family, was to get to the relative safety of the garrison house.

They made it to the door as the first shots sounded behind them. And in front of them. The village was surrounded. Samuel banged on the door. It was opened by a soldier, one of nearly a hundred sent a few days before from Boston, who let it swing open only after making sure it was white people banging on it. He rubbed the sleep from his eyes as the Morse family collapsed into the floor of the garrison and the door swung shut behind them.

The dull thud of musket balls hitting the door's thick wood could be distinctly heard in the garrison's silent interior.

Further down the street, Henry Adams came to the door of his home, gun in one hand, to see what the racket was. As he opened the door he heard a cry of "Indians" cried out. He recognized Elisabeth Smith and her small child hurrying towards the garrison house, then watched in horror as she stumbled and fell, her child underneath her. She did not get up. He turned to rouse his own family up, but was thrown back in the house by the force of a ball in his back, shot by an Indian hidden in a wagon bed in front of his home.

John Fusell loaded and reloaded his gun. He'd built his home with defense in mind, and now he made good use of the second floor, picking off Indian after Indian, one at a time, carefully leveling each shot. He'd learned early on in his years in this wilderness that methodical calm meant more than speed in gunfire. Ten quick, stray bullets killed no Indians. One carefully placed bullet often as not killed one Indian.

The Indians had hidden everywhere in town where a person could hide. As he fired and reloaded, fired and reloaded, dozens poured out of hiding places right in the center of town, with horrifying results to the men, women and children fleeing through the streets to the garrison house. He concentrated on those Indians who brutally attacked the children. He'd always had a soft spot for children.

But his accuracy did not go unnoticed by the savages. He heard battering at the heavy oak door of his house, but ignored it with a firm faith of the oak beam holding it in place.

It was harder to ignore the smoke that started to swirl around him. He glanced up to see his roof dancing with flames, flames which spread down the far wall and threatened to bring the whole upper structure down on him. He stopped his shooting and fought his way through the smoke to the stairway, only to find the first floor smoke heavier than where he was. He retreated to his window perch. If he was careful and steady, he might still get off five more shots before the smoke overcame him. That was all he could hope to do with his life now.

Those who made it to the garrison house stared with horror at scenes they glimpsed through the small slits in the wall. Samuel Morse clearly saw the smoldering ruins of his barn. As his thoughts had predicted, it had been one of the first buildings set to the flame. He packed and primed musket after musket, handing them to the Boston soldier next to him, who then leveled and fired into the street below.

The soldier, Edward Jackson from Cambridge, had never seen so many Indians. He didn't have to aim anymore. Fire downwards and he was sure to hit one. And he hit many before a ball found its way through the small slit in the log wall and into his throat.

Samuel Morse took over the firing, with nearly as much success as the soldier. Elisabeth Adams, a neighbor he'd known from church, took over his former task of loading rifles and passing them to him, repeating the routine over and over for what seemed hours, but in reality couldn't have been more then twenty minutes. Then Samuel Morse turned to get yet another rifle from her, only to find her sprawled on the floor, a bloody ooze in the middle of her back, and a horrified soldier a little ways behind her. He had been loading guns for another man at the back of the fortress.

"It… it just went off!" the young soldier said, holding the gun in front of him in awe. "I didn't mean for it too. It just went off." He continued to stare at the woman's body, sprawled out dead in front of him, while another man stepped up to Samuel's window to fire, and Samuel reloaded for him.

"Get back to your post, man!" Samuel yelled at the young lad, whom he judged couldn't be more than seventeen. "Do your duty now, and God may forgive you yet."

Terrified, the boy did as he was told, slowly reloading the first musket, then returning to his former speed, pausing every once in a while to glance again at the body that continued to lie sprawled for ten minutes before anyone could give to it the attention the woman deserved.

A loud cannon boomed from the main fort down the road, followed in a few minutes by another.

"Warning shots," one soldier explained to the villagers huddled into the safety of the windowless corner of the garrison. "We have troops in Dedham. Twon't be long before they all come marching over, and then we'll see how long the savages last," he said with a glee the townspeople could not share.

Outside the strongly fortified garrisons, the destruction of their town was nearly complete. Dozens of homes and barns were in flames. Cattle, grain stores, and some small stores of powder and ammunition were being quickly trundled away down the path back to the Indian camp. In less than an hour, despite the presence of over 100 troops, the town of Medfield had been turned into a smoky ruin.

By mid-morning the gunfire and flames slackened. For a while, all went silent. But the soldiers and villagers stayed in the fortresses rather than risk venturing into the smoky ruins.

"It would be like them," said Captain Oakes, who was in charge of the troops, "to have left a few men hidden behind, to cut us down as we head out the door." So they waited.

Another half hour and the sound of people on the march could be heard, coming from Dedham. The extra troops had arrived, and only now did the villagers and soldiers came out from the garrisons to greet them.

Samuel Morse led his family back to what remained of their house and barn. They passed a few dead bodies of Englishmen, neighbors Morse recognized. They also passed many dead Indians, Samuel noted with a vengeful pleasure, before arriving at the home site.

A few blackened, smoky, charred timbers still stood, giving a faint outline to where their home had been. The barn had collapsed completely. The shed next to it, filled with hay, continued to smolder a dense, heavy smoke. Samuel's wife grabbed hold of his chest, and she buried her head into his shoulder, sobbing.

"There, there, my love," Samuel said, thinking back now for the first time to the sprawled body of Elisabeth Adams, "We're the lucky ones, we are. The lucky ones." He turned her away from the homestead and headed slowly back towards the garrison house. There was much work to be done.

The Dedham troops, reinforced by the troops who had defended Medfield, stepped out smartly. With over 150 men, it was felt a quick pursuit might catch the Indian army on the road, and an advantageous assault could be had.

But no sooner were they under way than they spotted the smoky remains of the bridge leading to Sherborn, the only crossing over the Charles River for miles.

On the other side of the river, in plain sight, a group of Indians spotted the English troops, and began to laugh and taunt them, pulling from their bags plunder clearly recognizable from the homes of Medfield.

"Let's go back men," said Oakes, realizing there was no way across the river. "There's no more to be done here."

A young soldier approached the captain, a piece of paper in his hand.

"Captain, sir? I found this sir, tacked to a post in front of the bridge. I think the Indians left it, sir."

Oakes took the paper from the boy's hand. It was smudged from smoke, clearly pulled from a burning Medfield home. The lettering was crude but firm.

"Know by this paper," The Captain read, "that the Indians that thou hast provoked to wrath and anger, will war this twenty one years if you will - there are many Indians yet, we come three hundred at a time. You must consider the Indians lost nothing but their life, you must lose your fair houses and cattle." He folded the note and slipped into his tunic.

"It scares me, it does," said the lad, his eyes focused the Captain in an effort to keep himself from crying.

"It was meant to do that, my young lad," Captain Oakes said firmly. 'But I tell you this, if the Indians want to swap their lives for our cattle and our houses, I say its time to start the trading."

"Come along men. There's a lot of scared people back in the village who need to be moved out. We've got a long day's work ahead of us."

As the troop moved out, the young soldier couldn't help but look back at the far river bank. He'd never seen a dead person before today, unless it was all laid out in a coffin. But today he'd seen dozens and dozens, Indian and English. The note said this was only the start.

As he walked back to town he couldn't help but shudder.

Over the next days and weeks victory followed victory for us. At Groton, sixty homes were destroyed, and through the flames One-Eyed John taunted the fleeing English in words repeated over and over at campfires by the warriors who'd heard him.

"Watch what I do next," they would mimic him yelling. "My five hundred men and I will burn the following towns in order, Chelmsford, Concord, Watertown, Cambridge, Charlestown, Roxbury, and Boston itself." The warrior telling the story would then pause dramatically until repeating the final, self acclaiming pledge, yelled out as an anthem.

"What me will, me do!"

One Eyed John was not the only one flush with victory. Muttawmp himself was now predicting the English would soon be driven into the sea. There seemed no reason to believe otherwise. Although not attacked in the order so boldly predicted by One Eyed John (Canonchet's strategy precluded such foolhardiness) Weymouth was destroyed, followed by brutal attacks on Marlborough, Mendon, and Chelmsford. Worcester was also attacked and destroyed.

We had divided into three main forces. One, led by Muttawmp and One Eyed John, was made up primarily of Nipmucks and continued the fierce attacks on the ring of settlements surrounding Boston.

A second force under the inspired leadership of Quinnapin, who had married the Wampanoag sachem Weetamoo, continued the raids and attacks along the Connecticut River Valley first started under Muttawmp. Northampton, Longmeadow, and Springfield were all viciously attacked, causing further retreats among the English in that area, and further guaranteeing the safety of Peskeompskut, the vital base of supplies for the armies of the Algonquin.

The third force was made up of Narragansett under the command of Canonchet. Also with him were the remnants of my Wampanoag warriors, still valued for their skills despite their diminishing numbers, and still swearing undying primary allegiance to me, their leader and hero.

But I was not with them. Instead of accompanying my warriors in the shadow of Canonchet, I opted to stay with Quinnapin and Weetamoo in the West, staying in touch with all three forces in an effort to better coordinate their attacks. Matoonas consulted with me often, and acted as messenger to the other forces, often planning attacks with Muttawmp, who held Matoonas in much more respect than he did me. I flattered myself wise enough to use this to best advantage.

"What news?" I greeted Matoonas on an early April day. Matoonas was just back from travels to Canonchet's forces in the South.

Matoonas' face was wide with pleasure at the news he brought. "Providence has been abandoned. We again control the bay area."

"Come, sit by me, old friend," I said, patting the skin laid out by the cook fire next to me, over which a pot of chestnuts and herbs bubbled quietly. I filled a bowl with the broth and handed it to Matoonas, who appreciatively took a long swallow. It was the scarce time for food, and he had not eaten during the last day of his journey here.

"Now tell me the news of this great victory."

"Soon after the victory over the English at Central Falls, Canonchet led his men on to Providence. We were met before we arrived by a delegation sent by fearful English, who requested a conference for peace."

"What did Canonchet say?" I asked with interest. Despite the brilliance of his military leadership, I still had doubts of his underlying devotion to the war.

"He agreed to meet with them."

I nodded solemnly. This added to my concerns. "What came of it?"

"We appeared at the gates of town, nearly a hundred of us. Canonchet was dressed in his finest leathers, a bearskin, and silver powder horn. We were met there by Roger Williams."

"How is my old friend?" I asked, sincerely interested. Even with the war, I could not help but have a soft feeling for this wise, old, peace-loving Englishman who had once himself been banished from the militaristic Massachusetts Bay colony. If more Englishmen had been like Roger Williams, the war I fought now might have been unnecessary. It was my great regret that in the wave that had to wash away the Englishmen, men like Roger Williams must also suffer.

"He looks old." Matoonas answered. "Very old. It is obvious he has labored mightily to end this war. He leaned on a cane as he spoke."

"What did he say?"

"He said 'Welcome great Chief. I have heard of your bravery in the face of battle and of the leadership you have shown there, how you have continually confounded the best Generals of the English and brought them to humiliation and ruin. But now I ask you to use your leadership in another way. To bring about something harder to attain than a great battle victory. Peace. I talk not of a shaky, temporary peace, ending the fighting today only to have it erupt again next year. But a true, lasting peace among our peoples.' Canonchet then asked, quite simply, how such a peace could be realized. 'Through action,' Williams said, 'the action of peace. You have our town at your mercy. Show us that mercy. Spare Providence and shame the Englishmen with your strength and forbearance. Do this and together we will go to the other colonies and argue for peace. With your example, I feel peace can be achieved. Join me in this. You know me. You know I will not

betray you.' He stood there with his weight bowing the cane beneath him, begging Canonchet with his eyes. And for a few moments Canonchet was hesitant."

I couldn't help letting out a small snort. Matoonas noticed, but hurried to continue his story.

"Then Canonchet gathered himself, and, looking directly in the eyes of Williams, he stood and stretched out his arms. 'Your words are, as always, appealing, my old friend. I know you would not knowingly betray me And I know you believe what you speak, but I cannot help but disagree with you. What has been started can no longer be stopped with talk. Only battle will decide the issues that divide our peoples. This is now a war to the end. I will not rest until I see Plymouth itself in flames, for it is Plymouth which started this war with their attack upon Philip and his people. It is not on us that the blame must be given. You, the English, as a people, have brought this upon yourselves.' Canonchet then turned from Roger Williams and walked out. The attack began soon thereafter. By the end of the day, over a hundred buildings had been put to the torch, and the people driven off. Providence no longer exists."

I sat quietly, taking in this new information. It was the capstone in the recent string of successes the Algonquians had staged. But I could not help having mixed feelings.

"Do you not hear me, Metacomet?" Matoonas asked in confusion at my solemnity.

I displayed a strained smile. "Forgive me, Matoonas. Who among us could not be joyful at such news as this. The war has gone well, far better in fact than I even I had dared hope."

"Then what's wrong, friend?" Matoonas peered at me. I turned my face away, ashamed. "Ahh, I think I see," he said, nodding his head with a smile.

"What do you see?" I asked quickly, defensively.

"The war goes better than you hoped, better than you dreamed. But no matter how it went in your dreams, you were in the thick of it. You were at the head."

Matoonas looked at me, and I did not deny it. "And now Canonchet and Muttawmp and One Eyed John head the battle columns, and you feel your place is gone, your leadership wasted. But it is not, my old friend. Even the braves led by others speak your name with theirs. It is your vision they carry out. When stories are told by our children and their children after them, those who led in battle will be told of. But the highest praise will be for he who dreamed of the Algonquians as a nation, to he who labored for years to bring it about, when others had to be made to see what he already knew. Songs will be sung to your memory, Metacomet. Nothing can take that away."

"It is wrong to think of one's own reputation at a time such as this," I said criticizing myself, but I could not help feeling soothed by Matoonas' words. "Your concern is much appreciated. You are right, Matoonas. But the importance is not

that our children sing about myself, or Canonchet, or Muttawmp. The important thing is that they sing.

"Come, there is much work to be done. News of Canonchet's victory must be spread throughout the land. We must make sure it is used to inspire even greater victories of our people, of the Algonquin nation."

April 1, 1676

Canonchet settled back and took a long puff on his pipe. He let the tobacco smoke swirl around his head, alternately drawing in breaths through the pipe and from the smoky air he'd created around him, letting the soothing smoke bathe his lungs with warming vapors. Combined with the warmth of the sun's rays, and the fresh coolness of spring breezes, Canonchet felt relaxed for the first time in days.

It had been a busy time since he had returned South to his lands here on the Narragansett Bay. First had come the battle of Central Falls, followed by the sacking of Providence, and then continued raids on some of the smaller villages.

Now the battle must continue to be pressed. There was no time for wasteful relaxation. The loss of Providence would not rest easily with the Englishmen and would only prod them into further action. A large army would be sent out, intent on revenge. And for that, Canonchet knew he must prepare.

But with that vengeful attack which he knew must come, Canonchet sensed a chance for the stunning victory that might truly change the course of the war. Until now it had really been nothing more than a series of raids, some of them huge in scope and power, but still raids. For all the destruction that had been brought upon the English, Canonchet knew the tide of English domination had only been checked. It had not yet been turned. But the chance to turn it was upon them.

Upon him.

When the English attacked in force, he would be ready. He'd be waiting for them to stumble headlong into the series of traps he was already constructing for them. They did not learn, and he did. His defeat of almost 100 English troops at Central Falls had taught him much. He was getting ready to put the lessons to use against the attack he knew was forthcoming. Preparations were nearly complete.

But for a few moments, he allowed himself the pleasure of the pipe.

"The English! They come!" The young warrior gasped, breathless from his sprint into the Narragansett camp, as Canonchet came out from behind his temporary shelter, still clinging to the warm pipe.

"How many?" he demanded. "How soon?"

"Very soon. I saw them coming, not 100 yards from me. I ran directly here."

"How many?" Canonchet asked again.

"I can't be sure. A hundred. Maybe more."

Canonchet thought quickly. A scouting force? Certainly not the major attack he was figured was coming later. Not the turning of the tide. A force of 100 men could easily be handled, given a little time for preparation. But, if the report of the young warrior was true, time was the one thing they did not have.

"Abandon the camp!" Canonchet yelled. "Spread out into the hills. We will meet in the night at the little fork up the river. Tomorrow we will take care of this little party of the English. For now, flee."

Without hesitation hundreds of warriors who had been lounging in the camp sprang to action, gathering their weapons and organizing parties who would carry off the barrels of powder and shot they brought with them. It was a drill they had done many times before. Melt before the approaching enemy, only to reform and punish them upon better terms. It was a road to sure victory Canonchet had led them down many times before.

Canonchet gathered his coat and cloak more tightly around him, grabbed his flintlock, and headed towards the forest, but then stopped short at what he saw.

In the woods were Indians, but not his men. They were Mohegans and Niantics, Algonquin tribes still loyal to the English, even this far into the war. They were traditional enemies of the Narragansett who saw in the war an opportunity to punish their ancient and powerful foe.

Warning the camp of danger - Englishmen never sent forces to surround a camp before attacking - Canonchet turned again, heading for the river. Quick glances behind him showed him he only had a scant lead over his pursuers, a few of whom recognized him for the mighty sachem he'd become.

Peeling off his heavy bearskin, he ran for the river. He picked his way more slowly across the slippery rocks, intent on reaching the other side and scampering into the woods beyond.

But a rock gave way beneath his foot. He cursed as he went down into the water, hitting hard on the rocky bottom a few feet below the surface.

Stunned, he struggled to get up. But his clothes were soaked and weighed him down. He raised his gun to fire at his closest pursuer, a young Mohegan. But the gun did nothing, the water having wet his powder. The young Mohegan leapt into the air, hitting Canonchet in the midsection with his shoulder and pushing him down into the river.

Canonchet fought savagely, beating the young brave's ears and then wrestling free of his grip. But before he could get away more were on him.

In a few moments he was pinned. Then with two warriors holding each of his limbs, he was brought back to the camp where the English forces were just arriving.

Several Indians recognized Canonchet, and praise was showered on the young Mohegan warrior who had brought him down. Fawning under the attention, the young warrior approached Canonchet, now bound hand and foot, and still held by two warriors.

"Tell us, great chief," he said sarcastically, to the delight of those gathered around him. "Why do you run so? Why do you not stand and fight?" The gathered Indians laughed at the young warriors' brashness.

"Child!" Canonchet bellowed, and the laughing stopped. "You do not understand war!" Feeling foolish in the ensuing silence, the warrior retreated to a group of his friends. Canonchet looked around at the group. "I will answer only to your chief. Get him."

No one moved.

"Get him!" he bellowed again, and this time a warrior scampered across the camp to two white men huddled by a fire going over a crude map. There was a brief exchange, during which the identity of the captive was explained. The two men came over to the captive, staring at him for a minute before speaking.

"My name is Captain Avery. This is Captain Denison. We are the leaders of this army. I understand you wish to speak to us?"

Canonchet let the silence build for a moment before responding. "I have no wish to speak to you. It is that I will not speak to them."

Avery laughed. "I'm not so sure you're the one to be dictating terms here. We know who you are, Canonchet. Next to Philip, you're probably the most troublesome of the whole lot. Killing you will be a big blow to your tribes."

"They will manage." Canonchet said coldly.

"Will they now? Well I suppose they won't have much choice. That is, unless you're willing to give them one."

Canonchet eyed Avery suspiciously. Avery waited for him to ask more, but Canonchet stayed silent, and Avery finally began talking again.

"You see, Canonchet, I don't believe this war is in the interests of your people, and I have a hunch deep down you might not think so either. So I have a proposal. The rules of war say we execute the leaders of the other side if we catch them, but if you were to tell your people to stop the war, well then, I don't think we'd want to go killing an ambassador of peace. Would we Captain?"

"No sir, I don't believe we would," Denison agreed.

"Well then, I think that proposal might be something we give Mr. Canonchet here a chance to think on."

"No need to think!" Canonchet spat, and forced his way to his feet, throwing off his two captors despite the leather strings that bound him. "You offer my life in exchange for my people's capitulation. No thought is necessary. Your offer makes no sense. I am but one warrior of thousands. Kill me, and you kill one warrior. The thousands will fight on. They do not need me to destroy you. My death will only mean one less attacker in the next battle."

Avery leaned on the end of his gun barrel, considering the sachem's words. "I reckon you're right on one thing. Every Indian we kill is one less that might attack us later." Avery turned and looked at the prisoners captured in the attack. Three or four dozen Narragansett warriors were gathered in a clearing a little way behind them.

"Let's make sure they don't ever get the opportunity to attack us again," he said calmly, as if calculating a simple math problem. " Kill them."

With a whoop, the Niantics leapt into the clearing, and in moments the agonized cries of Narragansetts being clubbed and tomahawked rang shrilly through the air.

"What about him?" asked Canonchet's two guards, having regained hold of his arms. Avery looked at the impassive face of Narragansett sachem.

"Let him live. For now. Let him see what his arrogance has brought him. He may yet change his mind. Just sit him down there."

The two guards shoved Canonchet down on the ground, twisting his ankle and leg cruelly underneath him, causing the leather strings to pull so tight he quickly felt the blood leave his foot. But he made no sound. If he needed to find strength, he had only to listen to the cries of his warriors being massacred a few dozen feet away.

"Being found guilty of the charges against you, it is hereby decreed that you be executed, and that your head be removed from your body. The sentence to be carried out forthwith."

Without further comment Canonchet was led away from the hastily convened court in Stonington, outside to his fate. Faced with certain death,

Canonchet felt himself looking for some sign of harmony with the world, as the powaws of his youth had always encouraged him to. For years he had given little thought to their urgings, preferring the here and now to the ill-defined world of spirits and harmonies of the powaw. But now, faced with his own death, he felt a desperate longing for some sign of nature's harmony.

He found it in his recognition of Oneco, son of a Mohegan warrior who Canonchet had honorably killed in battle many years before.

"I ask that Oneco be my executioner," Canonchet said. There was some confusion as to whether this could be done, but finding Oneco more than willing to serve, both to revenge his father and to show good faith to the English authorities, an axe was found for him.

Hefting it to his shoulders, he awaited Canonchet's placement before him. Canonchet was brought to the chopping block, and took one last look at the world he was leaving.

"It is good the sentence is carried out swiftly," he said. "I shall die before I speak anything unworthy of myself." He looked again at Oneco, smiling in contentment at the completion of the natural circle he represented. Then he laid his head on the chopping block and stretched his neck far, giving Oneco a clear target. Canonchet had no wish for the deed to take more than a single blow.

Disconcerted by the smiling features of the great Narragansett leader, Oneco took a moment before lifting the axe above his head. But once in the air his blow was sure and swift, and all that could be heard after the sharp pop of the axe hitting the wooden block was the soft rolling of the Canonchet's head a few feet along the ground before coming to rest.

Oneco reached down and lifted the head high above him, blood running down on his arm. The small crowd cheered. A settler on the fringe of the crowd yelled out "He should have suffered like he made others suffer."

Oneco presented the head to the English authority, who took it from him solemnly.

"Be assured, Oneco, that this deed will not go unnoticed," the Englishman said. "This head will be brought to Hartford, there to be presented to the Governor as a token of the Mohegans loyalty both to him and to the King."

Oneco nodded his pleasure at the gesture.

And it was done.

The news of Canonchet's capture and death reached me a few days after the news of the victory at Providence, and as it spread through the camp, the euphoria that had come with Providence evaporated, replaced with a dull sense of impending doom, one that seemed to me far in excess of the news received.

"Why has the death of Canonchet so shaken you?" I asked the assembled sachems around the council fire held several days after the news had reached them. "It is a terrible loss, but we could not expect to win this war without loss. It is not a sign of strength of our enemy. They were fortunate to catch a small band unaware, and fortunate to trick that band and capture it. He was not killed in a great battle that ended in defeat."

"Mourn Canonchet, yes. Mourn his loss. But take from that loss not misery, but instead the flame of Canonchet's life. Hear his words when he died. 'You may kill me,' he said, 'But you will never kill my nation.' Think of the power in those words, the power Canonchet himself knew we have. Do not betray his memory with thoughts of defeat. Enlarge his memory by using it to inspire new victories and new successes. Take from his death a renewed devotion to our cause, and honor his memory by making the dream he saw a reality."

My words had some of their desired affect. The next day war parties were sent off for quick raids on villages and towns with Canonchet's name on their lips. Muttawmp, Matoonas, and One Eyed John met with me to further map out the plans and strategies envisioned by Canonchet. Within a few days Canonchet's memory still filled the camp, but it no longer haunted it. News of victories in the west and in the north along the Atlantic seacoast further revived the camp.

Early spring turned to late spring, also lifting spirits, as it brought with it warmer weather and better sources of food.

Supplies were still a problem I wrestled with every day. Battle plans called for keeping up attacks at heavy levels to disrupt the spring planting of the English. If their seed and fields were destroyed, they would have to give up even more of the towns they had settled, and as winter came again, hunger would become for the English a greater enemy than the Algonquians.

But disrupting the food supply of the English meant disrupting our own. Food had been scarce throughout the winter, but I had used the large reserves of the Nipmucks and Narragansetts wisely and carefully. Now those reserves had grown low, and if they were not replenished during this warm weather, the winter would be fatal to us. Even now, as blossoms appeared on fruit trees and fish crowded the streams, food was still short because of our heavy reliance on winter grains. Our corn was nearly gone, which meant maize and pone could not be made.

The work begun in the fall at Peskeompskut now took on even greater urgency. Spring planting began in force, with dozens of younger warriors sent to help the women and old men in the fields. Additional parties of older braves were also sent to fish the bounteous rivers. Encouraging reports came back of huge amounts of fish being caught and dried in the sun for storage.

Hunting parties were sent out to areas that had been burnt the year before in preparation. Long years of trial had well proved this method in which several dozen acres of forest were deliberately burned early the previous summer so that by this spring low growing plants and bushes had appeared, including berries, attracting game animals in much greater numbers than did a forest, where food low to the ground was quite scarce. For the next few years this area could serve as prime hunting ground until it too began to grow too big for its own usefulness.

The reports of the work at Peskeompskut and other similar but smaller camps did much to relieve the fears I harbored of hunger over the next year. But even with this effort so many warriors needed to be fed it remained a constant source of concern.

But real battle was now uppermost in our minds. As the showers of April slackened, my own attention turned to towns closer to the sea.

Sudbury - April 20, 1676

The town of Sudbury lay a scant seventeen miles from Boston. A few short months before it had stood firmly in the middle of the ever widening circle of towns that crept out from Boston's center.

But on this April morning it was now the outer ring, the first line of defense in what had increasingly become a war for survival against the Indian savages.

The news of Canonchet's death was ignored here. Everyone knew the force behind the Indian movement was King Philip, and good information had it that he was in the area, and would personally lead the oncoming attack.

And the town was certain an attack would come, either at Sudbury, or nearby Concord, or perhaps a repeat against what was left of Marlboro. But it would come.

For days the villagers spent their nights not in their own homes, but in the stout garrison houses that dotted the village. These had been fortified again and again until the villagers were confident they could withstand even the most menacing attacks. Troops were scattered throughout the villages in the area, ready to converge at once when the sounds of battle were heard off in the distance. Sudbury was not Brookfield or Deerfield, isolated and waiting to be attacked and laid siege to. When the Indians came help would only be a short march away.

The villagers were not alone in knowing their defensive strength. Muttawmp, through the aggressive work of his scouts, also knew the enemy had troops in several towns in the area. He knew the garrison houses provided for the villagers while they waited for help to arrive.

But he also knew his own warriors. And he had confidence in them. Had they not been sent off the morning before with the blessing of the spirits upon them, as revealed by the venerable Okeneco, the old and revered powaw of the Narragansett? Okeneco told the warriors the gods were with them. They would be invincible before the English toads. He filled them all with the hope and promise of great victory. And why should it not be so? It had been so many times before for these brave warriors.

So as morning broke, he ordered half his attackers forward into Sudbury to begin the systematic burning and raiding of the homes, barns, and cattle that were not protected by the garrison, and held the other half of his men back, setting them along the trails that led from the other villages to Sudbury.

Having brought five hundred men, Muttawmp's attack on Sudbury did not suffer from a lack of force. The Indians attacked mightily, whooping and shouting, burning, and pillaging, catching the few diehards who refused the shelter of the garrison, and killing them slowly and painfully in plain sight of those in the garrisons. Gunshots rang from the garrisons, dropping warriors on either side, but other warriors took their place, and the burning went on.

In Concord, a few miles north, the sounds of battle were heard and a dozen men, determined to help their neighbors, shouldered arms and headed out down the trail.

Less than a mile from Sudbury, guns still resting comfortably on their shoulders, they were attacked from behind by almost a hundred Indians. Those who weren't killed immediately were taken to a clearing a few hundred yards away and slowly tortured.

Another sixty soldiers from Marlboro shared a similar fate. Marching in formation, scouts on their sides to protect against ambush, they headed north to the sound of the guns. As they came around a bend, a log in the trail blocked their path. Captain Samuel Wadsworth immediately saw it for what is was.

"Fire and scatter!" he yelled, and his men, mostly veterans, followed his order as the log in front of them burst with flames and smoke. From behind the solid protection of a large oak tree, Wadsworth surveyed the carnage. Less than ten men down. He called for his scouts, who quickly came to him. They reported Indians in front, but not to their sides. It would be a straight up battle.

"Soldiers!" Wadsworth yelled out. "Prepare and load." He waited twenty seconds, mentally taking himself through the steps necessary to reload, then with a hard "Attaaaaaack!!" he raced out from his position towards the log and the Indian line.

He was followed by fifty men, holding onto their guns without shooting. Shooting at a run meant not hitting anything. Better to run and still have your shot when you reached the line.

As they came to within a few dozen yards, the log again erupted in flame and smoke. Wadsworth heard the screams of his own men as a few balls hit their marks. But a quick glance assured him his troop was largely intact.

The log was only a dozen feet in front of him now, and he saw Indians caught in the middle of the reloading process desperately ramming lead balls down their guns. But before they could level them the guns of the English crackled out with deadly accuracy. A dozen Indians died where they had stood, the rest threw down their guns and raced down the trail away from the deadly onslaught.

Wadsworth smiled maniacally. "After them men, after them!" he yelled, waving his saber over his head like some Cromwellian general back in Merry Old England. "The back of an Indian makes the best target!"

The men followed, vaulting the log, trampling on the fallen bodies of the Indians behind it, stomping to death those only wounded by the fire of the English.

The chase went on for a hundred yards, and several more Indian warriors fell from the accurate English shots.

"It's like a turkey shoot, sir!" one excited soldier said as he raced by Wadsworth. Wadsworth, a portly man, huffed and puffed from the exhilaration, and a large smile broke across his face, watching the two dozen Indians still running down the path.

And then they were gone. As suddenly as they appeared, the Indians left the path and melted into the woods.

Why hadn't they done that before? Wadsworth searched the forest around him, the smile gone from his face as he pondered the small hills on both sides.

"Retreeee…" he yelled before his words were cut off by what felt like a hand ripping away his throat. He reached up with his own, but only felt the bloody mass of soft flesh. He sunk slowly to his knees, as all around him the air sprung alive with bullets which shot down at his men from both sides, and from both front and behind.

A trick! It had all been a damned Indian trick. They were surrounded and outnumbered. Badly outnumbered. Already half his troop was on the ground, wounded or killed. The few that remained standing were now the ones caught desperately trying to reload. Wadsworth counted nine men tomahawked by painted Indians until he felt his own hair jerked harshly from behind and a cool, sharp blade find its way into what was left of his throat.

The report of victory over the Marlboro troop was a welcome one to me, but still I watched the battle for the town unfolding below me with concern.

More soldiers had approached from Watertown. Unlike the first two relief companies, this one had scouts and flankers that protected them from ambush, and they brushed aside the loose defense meant to draw them into a trap.

They marched into town proudly and with force, moving through the scattered Indians as a fish through water. Once they reached the garrison houses, the townsmen joined them, and together they formed a battle line that drove us before them.

Warriors who had been burning and plundering only minutes before this company's arrival now could not organize an effective defense against the smartly led attack, and I watched as they were beaten back across the river. Those who put up resistance or hid themselves in a barn or bush were routed out and killed. The day was threatening to become a massacre.

I hurried down the hill on the west side of the river, holding my gun in the air with my one scarred hand, yelling directions to the warriors coming across the brook and to others who, also seeing the change in battle, rushed to help me turn back the tide.

Bullets whistled past me as I approached the bridge and organized a line of defense. The river provided a natural defensive line, and in a few minutes I had used it to full advantage, halting the English troop, which now had the choice of either trying to rush the bridge and be cut to pieces, standing where they were and being cut to pieces, or retreating back into the safety of the town. They chose the last and, with our Algonquin defensive line firmly established, the threat of further attack from the English troop was gone.

We made our way back to our camp, joined now by the other warriors who had been summoned by Muttawmp, carrying with them a large load of supplies, some cattle, and several prisoners.

We had sacked the town, destroyed two of three relief columns sent to drive us off, and fought the third to a standstill. By any standard it was a victory.

Yet deep in my soul this victory felt different from the heady successes of just a few weeks before. The English, in the end, had been better prepared for our coming, had fought us off longer and protected more of their town. And while two victories had been won over the relief columns, the third column had marched into town without so much as a stutter.

Victory was still ours today, but thoughts nagged at my stomach about future battles not being so easy.

I saw it clearly. The English were finally learning how to fight.

It had been my fear all along. It was why I had urged the Algonquians to strike at the very heart of the colony, instead of its edges. In loss after loss the English had learned from us. It was a harsh lesson - taken into their stubborn hearts only after the loss of many lives. But the fruits of the education were now being seen. Fewer soldier companies and supplies could be caught off guard by ambush. No longer could towns be attacked by creeping into them unnoticed in the night.

And in this last battle, I noticed another fact which disturbed me more than the rest. Accompanying the soldiers that drove back our Algonquian forces at Sudbury were guides. Indian guides. Guides who knew both the territory and the tactics of the Algonquians. The English, who at first has imprisoned all Indians in their midst, even those long friendly towards them, afraid they too would become part of the rebellion, had now discovered their value as guides into the world of Algonquin war. These changes required basic changes in how we approached the war, and for the next several days I spent much time walking through the shadowy forests alone, thinking through what these changes meant and, more importantly, how the English tactics could be countered.

For they had to be countered. This I knew. More than ever before it was now a war to the death. Too much blood had been spilt for any other solutions. Either the white man would win, or the Indian. Only one would dominate. There was no middle ground.

But I still believed the Algonquin could gain the upper hand. If the English learned, so could the Algonquin. Dozens of towns had been destroyed. And while hundreds of warriors had been killed in battle, so too had hundreds of Englishmen felt the punch of lead, or a cold, hard blade of steel. We were weary, but how much more weary must the English be, who still could not claim one solid victory over the Algonquin nation they had treated with such contempt for so many years? Erasing my own doubts, I knew my next challenge.

At the next meeting of the council of sachems, as the victory of Sudbury was discussed and the loss of Canonchet once again brought forward as an ill omen, I stood again in the position I had occupied so often in the past years, exhorting and persuading those around me of the necessity of my views.

"We have had nothing but victory after victory," I spoke. The flickering campfire threw bright lights alternating with shadows across the faces of the gathered sachems. "Our enemies have been driven from their towns, and driven from their fields. They have felt the power of the Algonquin, and have learned to fear that power.

"Why then do we talk of defeat? Why, when I look to you, the men who have been chosen to lead your peoples, do I see nothing but gloom's long face? A year ago you believed the English could never be defeated in battle. But we defeat them

again and again. The Algonquin warrior has proved his worth. But now you would say though we defeat them in battle, we will never win the war?

"Where are the leaders of history? Where are the men to lead our nation in ways of which stories will be told in generations to come? Now is our time. Now is our destiny. The way has been shown to throw off they indignity of the past fifty years and recapture the pride and honor that is by right our own.

"The white men fear us now. They know we defeat them. Why then do you, who should know us better than they, have such doubts?"

I looked around the fire, and from the downcast eyes I could tell I shamed them. I was crestfallen. I wanted them to defy me, to scream their hatred of my words. But the men in front of me seemed beaten, and I finally left the fire without saying anything more, disgusted.

Outside the reach of the firefight, Matoonas caught up with me. "Do not let them concern you," Matoonas pleaded. "Haven't they always been against you? Haven't they always dampened your vision with their sour minds?"

"But what is to be done, Matoonas? If they will not lead their people, what is to be done?"

"It is simple," Matoonas said, staring as if the answer were in front of him. "If they will not lead their people, you must! The warriors are not disheartened. They know the victories they have are real. They know they can defeat the English. And they know you know it. They will follow you, just as they followed Canonchet. Even more devotedly, for you are their hero."

"I do not know, Matoonas. Their leaders may keep..."

"Since when does King Philip let the wrong opinions of misguided sachems stand in the way of what he knows to be true? You asked in the council fire why they should doubt the strength of the Algonquin when the English had no such doubts. Why then should you doubt the English as to who is behind this war? It is you, King Philip -Metacomet, to whom the warriors will turn. Lead them, and victory will be certain to follow."

Matoonas stared hard into my eyes, looking for the indignant fire that had lit my very being for so many years. Matoonas knew it would have to be rekindled if I was to exert the leadership he suggested I now take on.

"Do not take my word, Metacomet. Go out now, among the fires and the dances of the camp. Talk not with the moss-covered sachems, but with the warriors who have carried the fight. Then you too will again believe the words you spoke tonight."

With that Matoonas left me. I looked up at the stars, staring at their brightness in the cool, moonless sky, then once again brought my gaze down to earth, spotting the flickering light of a campfire far down the path.

I headed for it.

I could feel the excitement of the young warriors at having King Philip sitting with them, sharing their meager fare along with them and listening to their stories of battle.

One after another they rose and recounted in dramatic detail the deeds they had done, and the deeds they had seen others do. They spoke of their elation in victory, and their sadness at the death of their friends. But never did they doubt their cause, or that the battle should be pressed. They were confident of victory, and listening to them helped shed my gloom of the sachem fires. Matoonas had been right. The Algonquin leaders took a dark view of a war going right, and these men knew it.

I had sat for hours and was the beginning to think I could finally sleep, when one of the warriors called for another to speak, a call that was soon echoed by the others in a rhythmic chant.

"Kickamon. Kickamon. Kickamon."

As the chanting continued, an older warrior, seeing my confusion, leaned into me. "Kickamon is a Nipmuck boy. Or man, I should say. He has lived almost thirty years. But you will see why I call him a boy. He is no taller than a ten year old child, and no bigger either. He is too small for battle, too small for the hunt. But he has spent years listening to the tales of the elders, and knows them all well."

"Ahh, I see," I said, "He is a teller of the ancient tales."

"No," the warrior said. "He cannot repeat a single one. At least, not accurately."

I again looked at the warrior in confusion.

"He tells new tales. Fantastic tales that mix the old legends with the new. He weaves what happened yesterday with what goes on today, and, some say, with what will happen tomorrow. Among his own people he is a much respected powaw."

A small, misshapen creature shuffled in before the fire, his back to me for a moment, then turned quickly around.

I expected a face to match the body, some bent, craggy visage. Instead I found the face of a man, a proud man, with eyes deep and mouth wide. A face of wisdom. When he spoke, his voice came out like the low howl of a moose in the forest, steady and strong, full of power. I listened, transfixed.

"In the days of our fathers," the boy-man began, "Before the white man came to our shore, a moose and a bear came together at a watering place, each thirsting for the clear liquid, for each had gone long without drinking.

"Each watched the other as they approached, for each respected the strength of the other. But each also knew of his own strength, and was not about to back to back down. Still, neither dared take his eyes off of the other long enough to drink from the river.

"Finally the bear spoke to the moose, and said 'Go. Drink from the river. And once you have drunk from it, then will I drink, and then we shall neither be thirsty.'

"The moose trusted the bear's words and moved towards the brooks, for it had been many hours since he'd arrived, and his thirst was strong. But as he turned his head towards the cool water he sensed the bear moving behind him, and quickly turned back to find the bear near him, paw in the air as if to strike.

"The moose lowered his head and thrust his huge antlers forward to protect him from the bear.

"'So,' the moose said, 'I discover your treachery, and will no longer trust your words.' And the moose stood, with his hind end to the water, between the river and the bear, his mighty antlers poised to protect himself from the bear, and keep him away from the river.

"So they stayed for days, and then for months, each standing guard to the other, each watching the other to make sure neither drank. The thirst of each grew enormous, but the will of each was even greater.

"Other animals came to drink from the river, but seeing the standoff, went to another watering hole further downstream. Neither moose nor bear would move from their spot, for honor demanded they stay at the spot until the other gave in.

"Winter came, and the bear nearly froze because he could not hibernate. Spring came and the moose nearly starved because he could not eat. Six months had passed since the bear and moose had first come to drink, and yet neither had drunk yet, for fear wouldn't let them attempt it, and honor wouldn't let them leave.

"Then came the spring day when the moose shed one antler. And the moose knew he was doomed, for when the other antler fell, he would be defenseless, and the bear would win. As he stood there he saw the bear eye the one antler, and noticed the bear lift his paw, to be ready.

"The moose came to a decision, and without warning charged the bear with head down. Because he only had one antler left, the bear was caught off guard. His good antler caught the bear in the chest, pushing him onto the ground, and hurting the bear mightily. The other animals watching the contest all agreed the moose was winning the fight.

"But with only one antler, all he could do was push. He couldn't trap the bear between two antlers and grind one set into him to kill him. And if he stopped pushing for even a moment, the bear would regain its balance and swipe the moose with its mighty claw. So he continued to push the bear back with the one antler, using it both as a weapon and as a shield. He pushed the bear for a day and a night, and then another day, the bear howling with pain, but not killed.

"And then, just before the second night fell, the second antler snapped. Now the bear knew the moose was his, and without hesitation tore into the moose with a fury only the wounded know.

"In a few moments the battle the two had waged for so many months was over. The moose lay dead in its path, next to the fallen antler that had spelled out his doom.

"Within a few months all that was left of the moose was a few scattered bones. But the bear, who now could gorge himself on berries and plants to its stomach's content, had grown large and healthy. One day as it walked down the path where the remains of the moose lay, it thought back to the day both had approached the river.

"'What you did not know, great moose,' the bear said, 'was that I had watched you for years, and knew that every spring your antlers fell. I knew I would win.' And without another word, the bear pushed the remaining bones out of his path.

"Ever since that time, the bear has drunk from the river, and never again given thought to the moose."

Peskeompskut - May, 1676

The Nipmuck squaw leaned out over the frothy river beneath her, the spear she had sharpened so carefully that morning gripped firmly in her hand. She stared into the waters, and spied the dark, quick shadow darting below her. More from reaction than thought she jabbed the spear into the foamy water and just as quickly jerked it out.

On the end of the stick squirmed a thick, silver salmon, five pounds at least. The squaw looked at it satisfactorily, pulled it off the stick, and dropped it into a basket behind where it flapped through its final death throes in the company of nearly a dozen other lifeless members of its school.

The squaw's young daughter now heaved the heavy basket onto her shoulder. She carefully stepped off the wooden platform, built to give her mother a better place to spear over the smooth, slippery rocks that lined the banks of the river in this narrow gorge. She carried her heavy burden down the narrow, well worn trail to the village, where she traded the full basket for an empty one to bring back to her mother.

At the village the fish were boned and laid out over a bed of coals to dry by the older women of the village, whose eyesight no longer made them fit to spear the salmon at the riverbank. The work was repeated up and down the riverside, bringing in hundreds of pounds of fish in a seemingly endless stream. Each fish was boned and dried. Some were stored, others were taken down the trails to the battle encampments spread throughout the Connecticut River Valley.

The clang of the blacksmith's hammer was also heard in the village, as forges had been set up to repair weapons by Indians trained in the blacksmith trade under their former English masters.

In fields a mile away from the riverbank, old men, young boys, and most of the handful of warriors left to protect Peskeompskut were planting crops in rich fields and meadows which only the year before had been worked by the English farmers of Deerfield. They planted the precious seed sparingly. The winter months had drained their reserves, forcing them to eat grain they would normally have used for seed. But with careful planning and cultivation, a bountiful crop, enough to sustain the armies in the field and replenish the seed supply, could still be grown.

The workers could already taste the feast planned that night. A raiding party had brought back almost 70 head of cattle from the settlement at Hatfield, a few dozen miles off. Two of the cattle were to be slaughtered in celebration, and salmon would also be abundant, as it had been for several weeks. After a winter of empty bellies, food was plentiful, and the Indians couldn't wait to enjoy it.

That night the feast went on as planned, accompanied by dancing and songs. Several Indians from nearby villages came, and all joined in the festivities. A few kegs of rum, found in a deserted storehouse in Deerfield, were opened and many of the Indian warriors drank plenty, partly out of celebration, partly to counter the boredom.

"Why are we sent here?' asked one who had several turns at the kegs contents. "There are no Englishmen here to attack us. When have they ever left their precious forts?"

The others agreed. Some had been here most of the winter, and the only white men they had seen were captives brought back from far off raids. These captives were loosely watched. Several had run off, and the warriors who chased them down knew there was no settlement nearer than Springfield, forty tough miles off. Running off was the same as a death sentence.

The feasting and celebrations went far into the night. Honor was given to the warriors who continued to battle and win against the English intruders. When time came for sleep, even the few guards normally sent out on watch were allowed to rest instead by the warmth of the fires. This was Peskeompskut. This was safety.

Captain William Turner coughed once, and then twice, then broke into a fit of coughing that he smothered with the arm of his leather jacket, soaked through by the heavy rain.

"Ahh, Captain," noted the sergeant riding beside him. "I still think the place for you is in the sick bed."

"I've had enough of it, thank you sergeant," said Turner with a forced cheer. In truth he probably was too sick to be leading 150 ill-trained men though the forest on a desperate gamble. But the opportunity was there, and Turner had enough experience to know you couldn't depend on an opportunity to remain long, or come again.

So he'd risen from his bed and scraped together this force, not waiting for the experienced men promised to him weeks before. If he waited for them, they might all be pushed into the sea.

Turner knew the prize that lay up here. Only a few days before Jeremiah Williams' son Joseph had stumbled into the village, having escaped from the savages just a few days before. He told Turner of the huge Indian village settled on the banks of the Deerfield River. Turner listened as the young man described in well observed detail what he had seen, and Turner recognized this was a main supply base for the Indians.

More importantly, he knew the base was virtually unguarded. Joseph reported very few warriors, which made sense given the heavy attacks and raids carried out in the area. The Indians, Turner figured, probably felt no English force would attack so far north as long as the Indian forces were so active here. And Turner knew they were almost right. No captain he knew of would take on such a risk. No captain except him, of course. He could see great advantages to such an attack.

As dawn spread over the hills to the east, Turner's hunch strengthened. Ahead of them, to the north, wreaths of smoke wafted lazily into the heavy air. From the looks of it there had to be hundreds of wigwams.

Turner signaled for his troop to dismount. He picked a half dozen men to stay with the horses, and had the rest come up with him. He sent scouts out on his flanks to make sure he wasn't ambushed, then pressed straight ahead down the path with his main force. They crawled silently, the roar of the nearby falls covering any sounds that might come from their movement. About a half mile down the path they found what they were looking for.

Spread out in front of them was the largest Indian village the troops had ever seen. Dozens of wigwams were laid out in a well ordered plan. But not a single Indian could be seen. It seemed too easy, and Turner sent a few more scouts off to the sides of the camp to protect them from ambush. He carefully stepped up to the nearest wigwam and, with his gun barrel, moved aside the skin covering the opening and peered in. In the pre-dawn dusk he could just make out the two bodies, still asleep and undisturbed. He let the skin fall back into place, then signaled for his men to spread throughout the camp. The men broke into pairs and placed themselves at the wigwam doors, until most of them were covered. Turner turned back to the wigwam he'd peered into, moved back the skin, and opened fire.

The crack of his gun was echoed by the eruption of muskets throughout the camp as the Englishmen shot Indians in their sleep from two feet away.

Hysterical yells and screams cried out as squaws awoke to find their husbands faces obliterated by a musket ball, only to have their own screams cut short by a second shot or the duller thud of a musket stock cracking against their head.

The initial volley was over in a few seconds, and alarms were now being screamed out by those Indians who had not been shot in their blankets.

"Mohawks! Mohawks!" came the screams from one wigwam, and the yell was soon picked up from one wigwam to the next. "Mohawks! Mohawks!"

Turner turned to the soldier next to him and grinned. "Sweet Jesus, they think we're Indians too." Reloading his gun, he turned and leveled it on a doorway a few dozen feet away. Inside he had heard a man pick up the yell Mohawks, and now the man burst out of the stick hut, gun to his shoulder, still screaming "Mohawk!" He stopped on seeing Turner, confused by the presence of an Englishmen, then the truth dawned on him, followed by a lead ball from Turner's gun.

The next twenty minutes were hell for the Algonquin villagers, and a turkey shoot for the Englishmen. The English volunteers, although new to army life, were veterans of several Indian attacks. Most of them had seen their land and homes burned, their cattle driven off, their neighbors slaughtered and taken captive. Now, with their bitter enemy helpless in front of them, they gave no thought to mercy.

Old men, women, and children were shot or cut down with a sword as they tried to flee. Those Indians who did manage to scramble out of the camps were hunted down. The bushes were systematically flushed out by the English troops, poking at every one with their swords, shooting at every movement.

The few who made it to the river frantically pulled canoes into the water, hoping to escape on its swift currents, but soon Englishmen lined the banks, shooting at the exposed targets, and turning the foamy white waters of the stream into a sickly pink.

Back at the camp Turner, unable to completely control his men, still made certain that military objectives were taken care of along with more primal revenge. Two forges had been found, used by the Indians to repair their guns, and Turner made certain they'd never be used for that purpose again. He also set teams to work destroying the wigwams which stored baskets of fish and grain.

"Captain," a young soldier yelled as he ran up to Turner, out of breath, "I just come from over that little ridge yonder," he pointed to a small, low hill beyond the village edge. "I seen a whole mass of Indians coming this way."

Turner didn't have to think twice. His scouts had told him several camps surrounded this main village. By now some had undoubtedly heard the attack and were moving to do something about it. So far the victory had been a huge success. Hundreds of Indians killed, much of the food production ability savaged, all at the cost of one dead and a few wounded. But he couldn't let his success obscure his basic weakness. He was still leading a group of 150 men dozens of miles from any help or security.

"Sergeant!" he yelled. "Gather up all the men you can and start rounding up the others. Those red bastards are on the march, and if we don't beat them out of here, we could be in for a rough time."

The sergeant, a crusty old veteran of many Indian fights, didn't have to be told twice. He bellowed out commands to form up ranks, but was largely ignored. Instead the men continued to pick off the stray Indian they could flush out of hiding and destroy what they could of the village still left standing.

The sergeant started yelling and cursing, soon joined in by Turner himself, and they finally started to get the men in order when bullets again began to fly, but now they were aimed at the English soldiers. The bullets had a remarkable effect on discipline, and men now quickly formed up and began their retreat, suddenly losing interest in the last, smoky remains of what had been Peskeompskut.

The twenty men sent to retrieve the horses fought a quick, hot action with a band of Algonquin warriors during which several of the horses were set loose, but most were recovered. Still many now doubled up on their mounts, giving those riders an uneasy feeling as they started down the long trails towards home. The bullets still flew thick, and some men, convinced they had a better chance on their own then staying with the main group, which was sure to be followed, dashed off into the forest.

Those who stayed indeed found the going tough. Indian scouts, unseen in the thick forest along the trail, peppered the band with shot as it moved steadily through the woods.

The worst came at the bank of the Green River. Their horses were forced to slow in the shallow, swift current, and the men made easy targets for the Indians scattered along the ridge above.

Sensing victory was quickly turning into another defeat, Turner made a dramatic move. Gathering a half dozen riders behind him, he charged the slope from where the heaviest volleys came, scattering Indians from behind every bush and tree along the way.

The maneuver worked. For a few blessed minutes the men crossed the river unharassed by gunshot. Turner turned his mount back down the slope to his men.

Suddenly he pitched forward off his horse. He felt as if he'd been hit with a plank. He reached to his lower back and found it wasn't there anymore. It was a bloody mass of flesh and leather. As his head sunk forward onto his other arm, he heard gunfire from the Indian position rise in intensity. Then he heard nothing.

Samuel Holyoke saw Turner fall and knew he was dead. That meant he was in charge now, and he didn't hesitate. Reasoning the main Indian force was now behind him, he used the Green River as a natural defensive position, ordering two dozen men to dismount and take up arms, then sent the rest of the men, including those double mounted, on ahead.

The men who stayed behind held fire as the rest moved off across the river. The Indian force moved down the hillside, intent on following up a chance for victory. But as they approached the river's bank, Holyoke gave his command.

The volley erupted, cutting down a half dozen warriors, and sending the rest scattering for shelter.

Twice more the Indians came. Twice more Holyoke ordered his men to cut them down. Finally, after the third onslaught, with powder running short, Holyoke ordered his men to quietly mount up and then race ahead to the main body.

Sporadic gunfire caught the returning troops every now and then the rest of the long, plodding march home, but no more large forces contested their retreat.

Their arrival back in Springfield - tired, bloody, and reduced in number by almost a quarter - was welcomed with the stony, grim gloom that now pervaded every town on the ever shrinking frontier. Even when told of the tremendous victory won early in the day, the gloom persisted. The townspeople of Springfield felt they saw the results of the raid all too clearly. It had been Turner's idea, and anyone who still tried to support the idea was quickly reminded that it had been a mistake, a mistake that had cost Turner his life.

The destruction of the base at Peskeompskut prompted another gathering of the council of sachems by the fireside, but my words, instead of having a calming effect, only roused the sachems to even greater gloom.

"What have we gained in the war?" one cried to the heavens, one who before had been conspicuous only by his silence. "Instead of the greatness promised us, we are worn out and hungry, while our enemies have food and more men in the field. Our children are dead, while theirs grow in safety in Boston town. We are fools to continue. Let us sue for peace with the English now, while we still have strength with which to bargain. If we continue to follow him," he gestured to me, "There will be no songs sung about us, no stories for our children to tell. There will be no children left to tell or hear."

I read all too well the silence that followed. It was the silence of agreement. I rose.

"Friends, I am not to blame. It is not my strategies that have been followed. It is not my plans that have been put to action. But that is not the question before us. The question is where to go from here. Can't you see? Submission now means certain destruction. As long as we fight, we live. As long as we live, we have a chance. We have hope.

"Do you forget that we have won great victories? Yes, we have suffered a tremendous loss. But our victories easily outweigh the losses we have sustained. Can you not see that? To give up now is to throw away those precious victories. It would dishonor the blood of those who have died, including Canonchet. We must not allow dishonor brought to so great a name."

My words rang out but did not echo, the gloom was too deep. Another Narragansett sachem stood in cold contempt of me.

"You speak of Canonchet as if he were your own kin. He was not. He was a Narragansett. The greatest of us all. While he lived I saw hope. But now with his death, all I see is despair. It is time to end the misery. Time to end the forced marches we demand of our women and our old men. Time to bring peace to the land so our children may grow and make us strong again."

"That will not happen," I argued. "The English will not allow it. They may say they will, but they will not. It will be as it was. They will steadily take our lands from us. In a few years we'll have no where left to go. We will be pushed west to the hills and beyond."

"To the land of the Mohawks?" the Narragansett sachem asked derisively, and a cynical laugh swept through the council. "Aren't you welcome there? The great King Philip?"

The Narragansett continued sarcastically. "Why is it the English fear you above all? What is it about you that puts you above even Canonchet in their minds? Maybe we should do the English a favor. Give them the head of the great King Philip, whom they fear so much, and they'll let the rest of us live in peace. Eh? What say you, chiefs?"

"What's the matter, King Philip? Are your subjects too strong for you to control?"

"Shut up!" yelled Matoonas, rising with a rage I'd never seen in him before, not even in the heat of battle. "You act so strong now. Where were you during the battles? Where were you when the fight with the English was hot? You call yourself a leader, why did you not lead? Why do you not lead now?"

The sachem considered Matoonas's challenge coolly for only a moment before he responded.

"You are right. Leadership is what is needed now. And I will. Tomorrow I will lead my men to the English and make peace. It is so easy to lead a people into war. It is not as easy to lead them into peace."

"It is easy for a coward to lead them to surrender!"

The sachem pulled a knife from his belt and lunged at Matoonas. Matoonas spotted the move and swung his body left, avoiding the thrust, then kicked up and sent the knife flying out of the sachem's hands, before falling on him with his bare hands.

But others stepped in and halted the fight. For a moment the two sachems stared into each other's eyes with more hate than had ever been present in battle. Later Matoonas would bitterly realize this hate was so deep it could only doom the war effort. But no thoughts like that entered his mind now. He wanted only to kill this contemptible Narragansett.

The sachem shook off the others who held him. Those who held Matoonas, sensing a relaxation of his muscles, also loosened their grip.

"Tomorrow I leave with my men," the sachem said firmly. "Any who wish to may join me." He turned and marched from the fire. Several rose and followed. I watched them disappear into the darkness, the fire reflecting in my eyes masking the fire I felt at this betrayal.

By morning, most of the Narragansett had left the camp. Only a few, under leadership of sachems such as Muttawmp, who'd fought too hard to turn back now, remained.

I stayed in my wigwam through the morning, sucking on my pipe with ferocious breaths, stuffing thumbfuls of the scarce weed into its bowl.

Wootonekanuske looked on with concern. After letting my anger play itself out throughout the morning, she ventured to speak to me when she served some boiled groundnuts at midday.

"Isn't it best that those who's hearts are not truly with you are gone?"

"It would be best if their numbers were smaller, or if those left were stout of heart. I fear those leaving will further dishearten those who stay."

"But if more victories are brought their way."

"That would restore courage. But their leaders are weak and quaking. 'Canonchet is dead!' they whine. 'How can we win without him?'"

"Surely not all of them say this."

"Many are still strong. Muttawmp, as much as I have differed with him in the past, is a rock. He will continue the fight. Many others will. But many will not, and we need them all to be successful."

"Is it over then?" Wootonekanuske asked, echoing the question I had wrestled with all morning through the haze of his frenzied pipe smoke.

"No," I said firmly, and in my voice I saw Wootonekanuske take comfort. "As long as there is resistance to the English, it is not over. If we continue to fight, those who are now feint of heart may yet be recalled to our case. But we must fight. We cannot sit on our behinds and argue in endless councils that accomplish nothing. We must take to the battlefield again. As leaders we must face the challenge and continue what we have begun."

"You will lead your men into battle again?" Wootonekanuske asked with a mixture of pride and fear.

"I must." I pushed a few groundnuts into my mouth. "But not here. I no longer have the faith of those here. Nor do I have the knowledge of the countryside to lead effectively in battle. It is time to go home. There I will be able to rekindle the flame, both in them, and in myself."

Once I had decided on my path, I hurried to carry out my decision. I gathered my warriors together and shared my plans. They were glad to be going home. It had been a long, hard winter and spring since they'd left, and all longed for the sweet smell of the ocean's bay waters, and for reunions with those who had stayed behind.

Even my goodbye to Matoonas, friend through the winter, was short.

"I expect to be back in the fall," I said. "Victories there, and here, with the return of summer weather will bring out the Algonquin nation in force again. Be strong. Fight on."

Matoonas agreed, but could not stop the moisture in his eyes as I turned to oversee the last of his tribe's preparations.

With the news that I was returning to Mt. Hope, the sachem council had taken the turn I hoped for, once again starting to make war preparations. Blame for the bad times was placed on my departing shoulders. But I did not argue. Better the blame leave with me than stay to poison the activities of the Nipmucks. The blame would not stay with me when I reached home.

Our journey home was slow. Many who went with me were women, children, and old men. It was a movement of Wampanoags to our homeland, and while I wished to get there soon, the tribe could not be rushed.

That is until the scouts returned to me with news from home, news that made me hurry on ahead of my column, accompanied by my strongest and best warriors. It was news that cut to my very heart, worse news than if the entire tribe had been attacked, or even destroyed. For they had not even been attacked.

And yet Awashonks had surrendered to the English.

I sucked on the pipe provided to me by Weetamoo, sachem of the Pocassets.

"The news has not been good, my old friend," she said, not in accusation, but in commiseration. I looked towards her but said nothing through the thickening smoke. "We hear of more surrenders in the North. Ammunition is low. Tribes are running out of powder. When they are attacked by the English, they cannot fight back.

"It is not easy as it once was," Weetamoo continued. "The English have learned. No longer do they travel in tight bunches, ripe for ambush. No longer do they return down the path they came, so that traps can be laid with certainty that the quarry will come. No longer do they sit in their fortresses, waiting to be killed. They have become the aggressors, and many of us are too weak to resist."

She fell quiet. She had not meant to be critical. She knew I understood the situation. I harbored no illusions. "You've aged since I last saw you, Metacomet" she said. "The lines in your face are deeper, your eyes sunken into their sockets. But most discouraging is your bearing. You walk with stooped shoulders and rounded back. Gone is the noble stance that never failed to win admiration." I grunted in muted assent.

"Only the sound of your voice is the same, that deep, resonant sound that could have come from the roar of a waterfall." We sat quietly for a few moments.

"Events have turned against us, I agree," I said. "But it is not because the English are stronger. It is our own doing. They have not beaten us. We have lost hope. We no longer believe in ourselves. It is our own leaders. They said we could not win, and they have finally convinced the rest. We have won great victories. But with victory comes death, and deprivation. They have seized on that to convince the younger ones of eventual doom.

"We are winning!" I nearly screamed. " The English know this, and that is why they now fight so hard. Like the wounded, trapped animal they are, trying to survive. It is we who do not believe. We kill ourselves."

Weetamoo smoked and thought long on my words.

"What then do we do?" she asked. "How do we convince our own people of the truth of your words?"

I took a few moments before responding. "The same way we have always done it. We show them. We attack and win. My warriors still know we can prevail. Others are still with me from the tribes whose leaders have surrendered. They also know we can win. I can still field an army that can bring ruin to the English. It has been two months since we last tasted success. We must taste it again. Are you with me?"

Weetamoo, veteran warrior that she was, wife to the great Quinniapen, did not hesitate.

"I am with you. What is our target?"

"Taunton. It is strong, but vulnerable. A victory there will show the world the Algonquin nation does not give up so easily.

"Taunton will be where we again turn the tides of war."

Taunton - July 11, 1676

I now saw in real numbers the toll the war had taken on my people. Of the nearly one thousand people gathered in camp, I had only 150 warriors with which to attack. The spring and summer battles had carved away the camp until all that were left were women, young boys and old men.

I gathered those I could together and set off through the woods towards Taunton, and new victory.

My scouts had reported the troops stationed in Taunton were off on another of the Englishmen's increasing forays into the countryside. No longer did they stay inside their fortresses waiting to be attacked. For the last month they had actively chased our tribes, looting villages when and where they could find them, with increasing success.

And why not, when the Algonquin had lost the will to attack their settlements? But what other Algonquin leaders took as a sign of defeat, I was determined to turn into an opportunity. If white soldiers left a town, I would attack it while they were away, forcing them to come back and defend it as they had been forced to do in the spring.

So, in the hazy light of dawn, I sat with my meager band of warriors in the outskirts of Taunton, determined to make the white man again feel fear of the Algonquin. As the sun broke over the eastern hills I gave my signal, a loud whoop that rolled out over the horizon and carried its message to anxious, waiting ears.

Algonquin warriors rose up out of their places and, with a collective scream, fell upon the homes and barns nearest them. In a few moments the cries of awakened villagers mixed with the shrieks of the plundering Indians.

I personally led six warriors past the burned out remainders of raids carried out in the glory days of spring. For a few minutes those days returned as the crackle of flame was heard once again behind us. I led my band straight for the main garrison, intent on gaining as much ground as possible before the guns sputtered awake from inside, when I would settle my men into a short but necessary siege.

The gunfire that erupted from the garrison house was stronger than I had foreseen, but I did not worry. I signaled my men to cover, and scouted the best path to the garrison house, looking for a way to smoke them out into my men's clutches.

But it proved unnecessary to smoke them out. They came on their own. First a few, them more, then still more, until four dozen armed men formed a battle line and started forward.

This was no small village guard. This was a full troop of soldiers spreading out among the homes, barns and fences in front of my small band. In a few moments they would surround us on three sides, making even retreat a risky proposition.

I looked on in disbelief. My trusted scouts had been wrong. The troops were not out on the march. What had happened?

But there was no time to think of that. Bullets whizzed around me, filling the air with the hum of lead. I had to concentrate on the present.

"Pull back!" I called out. "Pull back to the fence there!" I pointed to a fence a hundred yards behind us, where several of my men had already started shooting. I jumped out from behind a watering trough and scampered to them. Others followed, but now they drew the soldiers' fire. Of the six men who had been with me, only three made it to the fence.

I clambered over the rails and dropped down behind, next to a man who's name I was not even sure of, so changed had my ranks become.

"What is happening?" I asked for a report.

"Soldiers everywhere. We were attacked from behind when we came in from the North. They must have known we were coming. Someone betrayed us."

A strong coordinated volley struck the fence posts around us. A few dozen feet away several warriors pitched backward. Three screamed in agony at having their bodies ripped apart by lead shot. Two others were silent in death.

I peered through the fence in front of me, and felt my stomach wrench.

Dozens of Algonquin bodies were strewn throughout the village, some dead, others wishing for it. A very few were still unhurt, squatting behind whatever protection they could find, afraid if they moved they would be dead too, and afraid if they didn't the English troops now approaching would flush them out like turkeys in a bush.

Betrayal, my warrior had said. I did not want to believe it, but what other explanation could there be? What only a few moments before had been a carefully planned attack had turned into a rout, with my attackers doing the running.

There was only one course left, one I hesitated to call for, because once started I did not know where it might end. I peered again through the fence. A hundred yards away the English were forming a second line of battle. They'd be marching forward in a few seconds.

"Run!" I yelled, my heart breaking. "Scatter into the woods. Meet at the village."

I discharged my gun a final time as the warriors around me scampered off. I followed, running fast, my body low and my head down to make a smaller target for the volley of bullets that screamed overhead.

I reached the wood's edge and veered off the path into the heart of the forest, the trees closing in behind me in sweet protection. I ran and ran, long after I felt safe from the English. I ran because I did not know what else to do. I ran in blind exhaustion until a root grabbed my foot and sent me sprawling into a mud hole.

I lay there, panting, listening for sounds of others, and heard none. Pulling myself onto my knees I wiped the mud from my face. I sat back on my arms, fighting to regain both my breath and my composure.

Betrayed? It was possible, I supposed. But more likely this was simply the new English warfare. They had learned. They no longer thought stupidly. They avoided ambush, sent scouts ahead, did not travel in large, single masses.

And they had learned to hunt the Algonquin.

That was what the attack on Taunton had been meant to stop. But it hadn't worked. The force that confronted me today was part of the larger force that had been hunting out Algonquin camps for the last fortnight.

And having fought off this attack, they'd hunt us even more aggressively. Right now the soldiers from town would be on the trail, scouting for the battle camp from which I had led my troops.

Which meant each minute was precious! A camp of 800 women, children, and old men could be feeling the hammer blows of English troops inside the hour! I pushed myself to my feet and began to run. I ran with purpose and determination. I ran to the camp, to warn, and to protect.

For it was no longer a war to win, I knew. It had become a war simply to survive.

We had split into four major groups, each striking off on their own to seek safety. It had all been decided within minutes of my return to the camp.

I led my group, mainly of Wampanoags who had been with me since the beginning, to the only place they wanted to go. Monthaup. Mt. Hope. Home.

"What will we do there?" asked Wootonekanuske as she walked beside me, our son running along the trail in front of us. It was not a question meant to criticize, but one which begged encouragement.

"We shall establish our camp, and our defensive position. The time for offensive action has passed for this season. We must begin to build again, for the future. We will fight the English when they come. And they will come. But we will drive them off and not follow. We fight now to be left alone."

Wootonekanuske went silent. "I worry," she said finally. "Not about the future. The plan is a sound one. And it will be good to be home again on the land of my ancestors.

"My worry is for you, my dear husband. Your face has lost its life, its vitality. You walk now with strength summoned from reserves in you so deep they leave no strength for anything else. You who have always been so warm and loving now speak to me only when spoken to, and then only in short grunts. You have not spoken to your son for days, the son who for so many years you had taken with you on even the shortest journeys, teaching him the ways of the forest and of men."

I walked silently for a while longer. "I am sorry. I am tired. I have not the strength to do all. I barely can do that which is now required of me as sachem, as leader of a people I have brought here, to this place. To ruin. And yet lead them I must. I must lead them until there is nowhere else to go."

"And they will still follow you," she answered soothingly. "For where you have led them is the only honorable path to have followed. Where else could a leader have gone with his people, but down the path of honor?"

We walked on in silence, and for a few brief moments her words brought comfort to me.

Later that morning the old powaw stopped on the side of the trail, and urged us to go on. He would only need a few moments rest, he'd said, and would catch up to the main party.

An hour later I sent back my three swiftest scouts to check on the powaw. They'd returned to say the English were half a mile behind, and the powaw had been found where he rested, shot through the chest as he reclined against a stump.

The news forced me once again to drive my people, first across a stream and then through a dense swamp to solid ground on the other side.

I sent a small party on down another trail, with instructions to leave the impression whole troops had gone that way. I ordered them to lay in wait for the first English scouts, kill them, then rejoin the main camp.

They did so, killing two scouts, but then encountered a support party as they skirted around the swamp. Four warriors had been killed. The others, after a harrowing chase through the swampland, made it back to our main group. By now the English had discovered we'd left the trail, and once again I set up my meager band of warriors in a defensive position to slow the chase of the English, as I pushed the rest of the group forward.

It appeared more and more a race that could not be won. Yet it had to be. Taking advantage of the delay my warriors gave, I again reversed direction and took yet another new track through the woods and swamp. This time when the warriors rejoined the group, they reported that the English had been driven back, and the path I had chosen had been well hidden.

As they walked, Wootonekanuske could not help but wonder what would happen once they reached Mt. Hope. What would happen when they no longer could avoid the English troops by hiding? Would they really be able to hold off the white man's attacks?

Stop, she commanded herself, then looked again to the silent, grim figure walking beside her. He has led the tribe all these many years, wisely and strongly, she thought. He has fought bravely and valiantly against the whites. Now was not the time to doubt or question him. Even if it meant she must die with him, she would not stray. He had made their life worthwhile, and because of that, their death would be worthwhile also.

But then she looked ahead, to the lithe young figure of their son who, even with the meager food and little sleep that was now the way of the Wampanoag, scurried and scampered up and down the line of the marchers, discovering anew the world of the forest, the wonder of the plant, the movement of an animal, each with glee and promise of the young.

Could his be death ever be made worthwhile?

Several days passed, and the scouts in the rear had not seen the English troops over the last two. Finally they had slipped their grasp.

Metacomet, Wootonekanuske noticed, seemed to relax just the slightest bit. He was still as quiet as a tree stump, but now he sat back in the evening next to the fire, smoking his pipe. He stroked the head of his favorite dog, who, gratified by this reaffirmation of the love of his master, curled at his feet. And the country grew more familiar, for they were now in the far hunting lands of the Mt. Hope village. Wootonekanuske began to believe a corner had been turned, and that life might start to regain some of the small, comforting habits it had lost.

But on the third night since the last sighting of the English troops, a small, hungry, bruised and weary band straggled into camp, a dozen men and a woman from the second largest Algonquin group to divide from the Taunton battle camp.

They had been caught by the English two days before, they said, with their backs to a river and most of their men gone off to raid a small outpost nearby.

The English had shown no mercy, killing women, children, and old men as they begged on their knees, pushing through the meager defenses thrown up by the few warriors remaining behind.

The raiding party had returned midway through the massacre, immediately falling on the attackers with a savage fury none had felt for many weeks. At first their fury drove off the startled English, but soon the white man's huge numbers, over three hundred, decided the outcome for good.

The ones who stumbled into camp had escaped only once the group had been totally destroyed. A few others might be out in the woods, making their way also to this camp, they said, but only a very few. They had seen themselves most of the group killed.

Metacomet merely nodded, then quietly ordered that the survivors be given what meat was left in the camp, and a warm place to sleep. Once they were gone, he put down his pipe and crouched before the fire. He ignored the warm muzzle of his dog's nose, and slapped the dog across his ears when he persisted, sending the mutt huddling into the temporary wigwam Wootonekanuske had set up.

Seeing this, Wootonekanuske herself went into the wigwam - out of her husband's sight, onto the warm bearskin she still carried with them.

She did not want him to see her tears.

Boston - July 27, 1676

It was as strange a sight as the good people of Boston could ever remember seeing.

Here, on this hot July afternoon, walking along the narrow neck of land that led to the main part of town, and then through the town itself to the Common where several farmers grazed their cows on this lazy afternoon, came a long, scraggly trail of thin, ragged, red men.

At their head was Sagamore John, a Nipmuck sachem unknown to most of the Massachusetts Bay leaders, who quickly assembled when word reached them of the group.

But the man directly behind Sagamore John was very well known. Unlike the other members of the band, his hands were tightly bound with leather thongs, his ankles tied in a way that forced him to march with short, halting steps. He was surrounded by armed Nipmucks, the only warriors with guns in the whole group, the rest having laid them down far outside town, keeping these three only to ensure the delivery of this most valuable parcel.

They came to a halt before the assembled Massachusetts Bay leadership. Sagamore John waited for the prisoner to be brought to him, then grabbed him by the shoulders and shoved him forward, tripping him on the ankle ties, and he stumbled into the dirt a few feet in front of the astonished white men.

"My friends," Sagamore John spoke in halting, broken English. "I am Sagamore John, great sachem of the Nipmucks, and friend to white men. I bring you my people to show our friends our truth, and also bring them this man they look for. He is Matoonas."

Matoonas struggled to his feet, trying to regain his dignity in front of the white men.

"Are you really Matoonas?" one small, wispy man with a shock of white hair straying from under his cap, asked. Matoonas merely stared at him.

"He is," another burly man said. "I remember him from many peace delegations. He's one of Philip's most trusted captains." The man almost spit the name Philip. "What brings you to this day, Matoonas?" the man asked, mocking the old Algonquin with his courtesy.

Matoonas turned his gaze to Sagamore John, who smiled like a dog hoping to please his master.

"Treachery!" Matoonas spat.

Sagamore John's smile disappeared and he lunged at Matoonas, knocking him down again. "It is you who betrayed us," Sagamore John seethed, "by leading us into a war we could not win."

"Coward!" Matoonas sneered in Algonquin, and Sagamore John fell on him again with almost lunatic fury, hitting the tied figure over and over until Matoonas lay flat on the ground. Only then did Sagamore John remember his English onlookers and quickly rose, bowing as he did so.

"He is yours, now" he said, regaining his breath. Matoonas struggled to his knees. Two English soldiers grabbed each arm and dragged him to his feet.

"What shall we do with him, sir?" the soldiers asked.

The man addressed looked carefully at Matoonas. "It might be simple," he said, and took a step toward the prisoner. "Tell me, you are Matoonas, Algonquin sachem, leader of the attack on Brookfield?"

Matoonas said nothing, but his slow forming smile told the man all he needed to know.

"Take him down there," he said pointing to a large tree farther along the common, "Tie him to it, and shoot him."

The soldiers wasted no time. They dragged the large Indian between them down to the appointed tree. Within a few minutes Matoonas had been tied to it, while a large crowd of Boston townspeople gathered as word spread that the savage Matoonas was a captive.

Behind the Boston crowd stood the 180 Indians brought in by Sagamore John, staring at the scene in wide eyed amazement. Most knew that in surrendering both themselves and Matoonas, Matoonas stood little chance of being allowed to live. But having it done here, before their eyes, within a few moments of their surrender, was upsetting. It went against even their accommodated idea of honor. They began to eye Sagamore John, who had cajoled them into this course, with suspicion.

Sagamore John was also taken aback by the quick turn of events, and sensed the anger of his people. But he also sensed their weariness and resulting weakness, and felt they'd still submit if given the proper example.

So, stepping up in front of the crowd, he again addressed the white leader.

"I ask one favor, as a symbol of the lasting friendship between our people that I hope this begins," he said. The leader turned to him, waiting. "Let me kill him. It is right that is should be so, we who so wrongly followed him will now make right our wrong."

The white man considered this for a moment, then shrugged and nodded to the soldier next to him, who handed his gun to Sagamore John. He took it, leveled it at the embittered face of Matoonas, lowered it so that it aimed instead at his chest, and fired.

I chewed on the smoked fish absently, not noticing the taste of this precious meal, eating only to satisfy the pang of hunger I'd awoken with in my stomach that morning.

One advantage gained by the move back to the bay near Mt. Hope was the availability of fresh fish, assuaging the hunger that had become the constant companion of my Wampanoags. Game also improved, as warriors once again hunted the paths we knew so well, visiting spots undisturbed for almost a year, and therefore plentiful.

But corn was scarce. We had found a few of the old storage areas undisturbed, but most had been destroyed. What remained was needed for seed in the spring planting, nine months away. Until then, winter's starvation threatened to finish what the English had begun.

The last few days had also brought me disheartening news from the other Algonquin tribes. After seeming invincible in the spring, the various Algonquin tribes now offered almost no resistance at all, surrendering to any English troop that stumbled on them.

But the worst news was of Matoonas. He was betrayed by his own tribe, offered to the English in an abject show of cowardice. The very thought of the treachery enraged me and, as so often happened now, caused me to lose even the small appetite I'd woken with.

"I am going out," I said to Wootonekanuske, who was preparing a meal for our son, still snugly sleeping in the corner of our temporary shelter.

"You have not eaten nearly enough," she protested. "Stay and eat with your son when he awakens. He misses his father's company."

I looked at the sleeping figure of my son, and for a moment felt my grim features soften.

"He will sleep for a while longer. I shall return soon and eat more with him." I turned to my wife in a forced show of good humor. "Will that be satisfactory?"

Wootonekanuske smile and nodded, and I left the tent, exhausted by my show.

I wandered down the trail leading to the river edge and sat on a stump, absently tossing blades of grass into the slow, steady current of the Taunton River.

We were back to where it had all started. Muttawmp still fought on in the North, Quinnapin fought in the West. Here I led the fight, joined as ever by Weetamoo. But the fight now was to stay alive, and the English knew this. They were bolder and stronger. Their soldiers had been joined by new soldiers, anxious to take part in a fight that now looked so promising.

I tried to touch the time when the tide had turned, when victory had become defeat. We had won battle after battle, and then suddenly we had lost the war. It made no sense. But it was what had happened.

Perhaps the time had come to give up.

"No! Don't shoot! He is one of my own men!"

I looked up across the Taunton River towards the voice that yelled out. Standing on the opposite shore was a small party of English men, one whom I recognized as Ben Church, accompanied by a few Indians. It had been an Indian who had yelled. But now he realized his mistake and raised his gun to his shoulder.

I heard the explosion of the gun as I dived off the stump onto the ground. The bullet whizzed through the air above me, plunking itself into a tree a few yards in front of me.

I rose to my feet, but kept low to the ground and zigzagged my way into the woods, hearing the discharge of several weapons and the thunk of lead ripping into tree trunks nearby.

Circling through the woods I came again to the riverbank fifty yards further up, spying through the bushes to see my pursuers. Already several were in small boats coming across the river. Others pulled boats into the river to join them. In all, at least fifty men were crossing.

I ran back to the village.

"They come!! They come!" I shouted as I entered the just waking camp. "Hurry! Run, before they take us!"

Around me Wampanoags gathered their weapons and melted into the forest. I sent Wootonekanuske and our son off with others down the trail while I stayed behind. I gathered a dozen of the younger braves and ordered them to shoulder the heavy baskets of grain that were so important to the spring planting.

"Take them safely away, hide them, and make your escape. Remember where you hid them, and we shall return for them later." The boys did as they were told.

I organized the remaining warriors, only two dozen, into a defensive line along the trail I expected the English to follow. For several minutes we waited. Then down along the side of the trail, carefully using the forest as protection, came a half dozen English soldiers. I waited until they were within a few dozen yards of our position, then I opened fire, followed by the other warriors.

The soldiers, startled but unhurt thanks to the dense trees, scampered off, and my men and I reloaded, waiting for the full attack.

When it came, it came not from in front, but from behind, and was pressed only by a dozen men. But surprise and position forced me and my men to flee for our lives in every direction.

I ran through the woods. Englishmen were now spread out all through them, springing out from behind bushes and ditches to surprise braves who ran from the enemy behind them into the enemy in front.

I changed my own path. There was no helping the others. To find them would only draw attention to them. Instead I spied a small ditch out of sight of all but those within a few feet of it, and hid.

I stayed there for most of the morning, gun drawn up next to me, the finger of my scarred hand on the trigger. But though men combed through the forest several yards away from me, none came close enough to cause me to fire.

After hearing no sounds for over an hour, I crept out of my hiding spot and carefully made my way back to the place where the Englishmen had left their boats. They were gone.

I started to search for what was left of my tribe.

In a clearing a few miles back from the stream's edge I found where many of the tribe had gathered. Several paths through the forest led here, making it a natural gathering place.

I wandered through the makeshift camp, observing the grim, determined faces of my people, already remaking their daily life after the interruption of the attack. These were a people who'd grown used to adversity and deprivation, people made hard by the events of the past year.

I searched for my own wife and child, with a growing ache in my heart, and a gnawing in my belly, for none had seen them in their hasty flight from the river camp.

Then I came upon Lakeeta, an old woman who had with her an infant, the son of her daughter who had died during the winter. When I asked if she'd seen my family, her eyes grew sad and she nodded.

"Are they dead?" I questioned softly, not wanting to hear the answer, but needing to know.

"No," the old woman said, and for a moment my heart swelled with hope. "But they have been taken. The English captured them."

"Both of them?" I could hardly believe the news. "They captured both?"

"At first they held only your son, but Wootonekanuske came to his aid, knocking down the soldier who held him. But other soldiers came, and both your son and Wootonekanuske were taken. They are captives"

Captured Indians did not fare well with the English. Those who did not die, either after a sham trial such as that of Tobias, or from being held in disease-ridden captivity, were sold off to the West Indies as slaves, a fate I considered worse than death. And the wife and son of King Philip would get no mercy in such matters.

Inside me, a flame went out.

After all the death I had seen, and of all the fates I had contemplated, this was one I had never allowed myself to imagine. For my entire adult life Wootonekanuske had been with me, supported me, cared for me during the long years of trying to forge a coalition among the tribes. She had been someone I could turn to, talk to through my low moments, someone to celebrate my small victories with, small victories no one else would appreciate. Our son had reinforced our union, had given me a sense that even if I were to die in battle, I would in some important sense live on.

Now that was all gone.

"My heart breaks," I said to myself as much as Lakeeta, then fought to regain control of my jaw and fight back the moisture welling up in my eyes. "Now I am ready to die."

Taunton - August 6, 1676

Indians came in every day now, giving themselves up to the first white person they found. Men in the camp were getting used to Indians swearing allegiance to the king and begging for forgiveness for the war. Most would then ask to be brought to the commander, there to again plead their new allegiance.

It was so common they weren't brought to the Captain, absent a special reason. Elihu Washburn felt he had a special reason.

"He says he can lead us to Philip," he told his sergeant. The sergeant eyed the Indian with suspicion.

"Ask him why he would lead us to his own sachem."

Washburn talked the Algonquin language with the Indian who, with broad smiles and bowing gestures, answered in rapid dialogue.

"He says he has seen enough killing. The English have won. It is time to stop the killing. He says that since the taking of his wife and son, Philip's hate will not be stopped. He only leads them all to death."

The sergeant mulled this over, then decided only that it wasn't his decision. "Stay here," he told Washburn, "and keep a close eye on that red devil. I'm going to the captain."

Within the hour Washburn was in a party of twenty led by the Indian he had brought to the sergeant, heading down paths Washburn wouldn't have known existed without this Indian's guiding presence.

Smoke could now be seen rising over the horizon, and the Indian told Washburn that was the sight of the camp.

"Ask him again if he's certain King Philip is there."

Washburn talked with the Indian, then turned back to the captain. "He will say only that Philip was here last night, visiting Weetamoo. It is Weetamoo's camp, not Philip's. But when he left Philip was there."

The captain grunted. "Philip and Weetamoo. Now wouldn't that be a nice couple of prizes. The King and his Queen. She's almost as bad as he is, if you ask me. Well let's go, then. Even if Philip has left, Weetamoo is more than worth the effort. Washburn, take a few men with you and to the left of the smoke. Choate, you do the same on the right. I expect they'll try to run when we attack. Keep them penned in."

"Yes sir," Washburn said, pleased at the minor command. He'd never been put in charge of other men before.

"Move along men," he ordered the other three, once they were out of the Captain's hearing.

"Christalmighty, Washburn. Just because you talk Injun don't give you no right to boss us around," a soldier named Hunt said with a grin. "We know what we gotta do without you giving us orders."

Feeling a little foolish, Washburn shut up, but he made sure to go first through the forest, and the other men fell in behind him without another word. He was, after all, in command.

The gunshot signaling the start of the attack was followed by yells and screams, but no more rifle fire, and Washburn and his men waited for four or five anxious minutes before slowly advancing toward the camp, unsure of what had happened.

When they reached the smoke, it became clear. These Indians had given up without a fight. Several dozen stood in a small area, surrounded by a ten soldiers with muskets primed and cocked, but none looked as if they were planning on going anywhere.

As Washburn walked into the clearing, the Captain looked up.

"Did you get her?" he asked.

"Who?" Washburn replied.

"Aww Jesus. Weetamoo! She ran when we attacked. Ran down where I put you, blast it! Go get her!"

Washburn stood awkwardly, not understanding. "What about Philip?"

"He ain't here. Left this morning, according to these folks," the Captain pointed off to the prisoners. "But dammit, Weetamoo was here, and scampered off. I figured she'd run smack into you. But you're here, and she ain't. So find her!" The Captain was red with anger now. Washburn and his men lost no time in beating it into the woods, intent on hunting down the Pocasset sachem.

Weetamoo caught her foot on a root and tripped, but almost as quickly sprang back up. She could hear soldiers in the woods behind her. She didn't have much time, but she also knew these woods. She'd grown up in them, and they were her friend. She knew she could stay ahead of the soldiers for a time.

The attack had completely surprised her. She'd thought the camp, surrounded by swamps, was safe from ambush. Unless they had been led. Philip had warned her only this morning that many deserters were leading the whites to camps. The Algonquin were turning on themselves.

Others had surrendered, but Weetamoo knew she had to run for her life. She'd heard of Matoonas' fate, and remembered also the fate of Canonchet. Her own fate in the hands of the English would be no better. There was no honor in such a death. So she ran.

Her plan was simple. Find Philip and join him. He would fight on until the very end. He had to, of course. There was no other reason to live. He had asked her to join with him. But she had hesitated. The end was now obvious, and she questioned the wisdom of more fighting.

But now his fate had become hers as well. All she could do was join him and face the fate which must befall them, to meet it with dignity in battle, so that the spirits of their ancestors and the legends of their children would be served.

But she first had to find Philip, and that meant crossing the Taunton. She reached the riverbank and she looked across to the other side. To reach it meant to be free. But it was a long way to the other side, and the current was strong here. Better to cross down further where a bend in the river slowed the current, and the distance across was not so wide. She turned down the river path, but heard again the soldiers behind her. They were on the path, and would follow it. Her chance was in front of her, and without further hesitation she waded into the river, stretched out, and then brought first one hand over, then another, pulling herself through the water.

Even in the August heat the river was cold, and by the middle of the stream she felt her limbs tire. The current pulled her downriver. She no longer heard the soldiers on the bank. She tried to rest in the river, floating in the water as her father had taught her so many years before. But the strength of the current pushed her under as well as down, and she sputtered as her head was forced underneath. There could be no rest.

She again brought her arms up over her body, willing them through the murky water. But the current here was even swifter, and despite many long, hard thrusts, the western bank came no closer.

Now she pulled at the water just to keep her head above it, gulping for air, swallowing water in with it. Spitting it out took more concentration, and she felt her legs pull underneath her. She tried pushing them behind her to where they would push her through to safety, but she could not make them respond.

She felt the current slacken and looked up, hoping to see the bank. It was still a hard swim away. She pulled with her arms, and finally began moving towards it. But her strength failed her. She looked behind her, hoping the shore she left might be closer, within reach. It was farther off than the safe shore.

She thrashed frantically, trying to propel her body through the water, forgetting in her panic even to raise her head above it, concentrating all her strength on pushing herself towards the shore. She pushed and pushed, until her chest nearly burst from lack of air. Only then did she push herself upwards to break through the water to where her lungs could pull in the air.

The shore was closer, but still too far. Her arms gave out, and as she gasped desperately for the precious air, water flowed into her mouth instead. She could no longer spit it out. It filled her mouth, then her lungs. She grabbed with her hands for the air as if it were a ladder, trying to pull herself from the water's grip.

In a few moments, even her hands only grabbed water.

The discovery of Weetamoo's body, found on a riverbank by an English party, but reported to me by my scouts, did nothing to hurt my spirit. That had already been destroyed. There was no spirit left to hurt. Weetamoo's death was another inevitable and unavoidable turn in the path I now followed.

But to those who followed me, it was a blow as shattering as any they had thus far encountered.

That evening, as the darkness descended on the remnants of the tribe around a dozen different campfires, the tribal leaders, most new to their role having replaced others who'd fallen in battle, began again to talk of the future.

Wrapped in a blanket, I slowly rocked back and forth only a few short feet from one of the fires. Lately I could not keep warm, no matter how many blankets or how close to the fire I sat. I rarely took part in these discussions now, and even more rarely made decisions for the tribe, although the few I made were instantly obeyed. But the tribe saw toll the capture of my wife and son took on me, and combined with the defeats and setbacks which scouts brought news of every day, I knew they whispered their quiet, mournful doubts of my ability to lead any more.

Tonight, as on other nights, they talked of the best places to camp next, the best places to send a hunting party in the now desperate efforts to prepare for the winter hunger, and guessed the whereabouts of the English soldiers that scoured the land for King Philip. But, unlike other nights, the death of Weetamoo dampened the discussions until the warriors grew silent in despair.

"Perhaps," suggested one of the younger members, after the silence had lasted long enough to see the moon move through the sky, "It is time to surrender."

Silence greeted the suggestion, but no one spoke against it and, emboldened, the brave continued. "We struggle to stay alive, hoping to survive until winter. But what will winter bring? Hunger. Starvation. Death and disease. By avoiding the English we seal our fate as surely as if we now attacked Boston. Our destiny is set. Why should we suffer, if only to die?"

The silence returned. Then, without warning even to myself, I leapt from the flickering shadows next to the campfire like a huge bat flying through the air.

I grabbed the speaker by the neck and pressed hard against his throat, cutting off the man's air and stifling any screams.

The brave tried to break my bear-like grip, but I rose on my knees for leverage, and with savage thrusts I methodically beat the brave's head against a rock on the ground. Again and again I heard the sickening crack of the brave's skull against the unbending rock, until his body went limp. Even then I continued my stranglehold. No one dared interfere. No one dared breathe.

Finally I rose to my feet, pulling the lifeless body up with me, and then shoved it down onto the ground with contempt.

"Death comes to us all," I said loudly. "Let us meet it like men, and not," I said looking down at the body beneath me, "like whimpering dogs." I strode off into the night.

I watched what happened next from a short ways off. The camp remained silent for a moment more, then I heard a stifled sniffle. I could make out Alderman, brother of the man I had killed, struggling to hold his tears. He went to his brother and gathered the lifeless body into his arms, the head smearing him with blood and brain as he wept over him. Then he laid his brother down and crawled off into the darkness, still muffling his sorrowful sobs. I should have felt pity for him, but I did not. I had none left.

The next day I led us home to Monthaup. I again resided in the sturdy wigwam I had spent so many years in, but now I did so alone. Others also occupied their old homes, repairing them with material taken from homes that remained empty, a silent reminder of all that the tribe had endured in the year since we had left this place.

I stayed away from the nightly fires, remaining in my wigwam, alone and undisturbed. The killing at the campfire was never mentioned, and when Alderman disappeared from camp after the first day, nothing was said of that either.

Those that did gather around the campfires knew there was little hope left. They knew Monthaup was a trap, just as certainly as it had been a year before when they had brilliantly fought their way out of it, defeating the English for the first time. The story of that victory was told and retold now, in stubborn affirmation of their own worth as warriors.

The difference was they now numbered in the dozens, rather than the hundreds. Every day one or two more slipped from the camp.

Still I found myself clinging to small signs of hope. Thanks to a year's absence, the fish and game was more plentiful than we had dared hope, and some stores of grain had been recovered from hiding places undiscovered by the English invaders. Some of it was still good for bread. While still facing a hungry winter, especially if it was a harsh one, hope rose among the tribe that we might yet survive it.

Monthaup (Mt. Hope) - August 12, 1676

Many Wampanoags slept a sounder sleep than they had in two days, with bellies full and quiet hope in their hearts. But just beyond the small camp, danger found its way to them.

For Alderman had not merely left Metacomet, but in his hatred, found his revenge. He now guided the English soldiers to the Wampanoag camp, giving information on the size and defenses.

Leading the English was Benjamin Church, the same Benjamin Church who had faced Philip so many months before in the pea field. He had fought on since that day, learning the Indian tactics of war until he had become the most skilled of all English captains.

Now a major, he again made use of those tactics, spreading his men out around the camp before allowing any attack. He sent Alderman with a young soldier named Cook to the far side of the camp, where the paths led to a swamp, a likely escape route. Others were posted along other paths and trails, ready to pounce on those who tried to run.

But before he could ready his main assault, a shot rang out on his left flank. One of his scouts had stumbled on a sentry, who got off a warning shot. Immediately the camp in front of Church rose in battle hardened readiness.

But Church was also battle hardened. He stepped forward, saber thrust in the air.

"Charge!" he yelled as he ran down the path to the village. Behind him the English soldiers took up his cry and followed.

Grabbing my gun at the sound of the first shot, I rushed from my wigwam. Up the trail I saw the onrushing English troops. I ran wildly through the camp, waking those who still slept, urging others to make a stand, but make ready to run if necessary. It was soon necessary. The English onslaught was too strong to be withstood in a camp that afforded little in the way of defensive position.

"To the swamps!" I called, and ran down the trail. As I ran, bullets whizzed over my head harmlessly, and I smiled for a moment as I spied a member of my tribe standing tall on the path ahead. But the smile left me as I recognized Alderman. The incident near the fire came back to me, his brother's face rose clearly in my mind. I stopped in my tracks.

Next to Alderman an Englishmen rose and, seeing me standing in the path in front of him, did what he was trained to. He raised his musket to his shoulder and pulled the trigger.

All that came was the soft click of flint against metal. The spark failed to ignite the dew-dampened powder he'd neglected to keep dry. Alderman stood staring uselessly, his gun in front of him. Realizing what had happened, I felt a surge of the old fury and, pulling my knife from my belt, I charged at the two men who stood so still in front of me, my knife raised high in the air. For you Wootonekanuske, I thought, for you and for our son!

"Shoot, dammit," Cook yelled at the Indian next to him, and grabbed for the gun Alderman held awkwardly in front of him. But as he laid his hands on it, Alderman jerked it back from him and, raising it to his shoulder, took a bead on the onrushing Wampanoag sachem he recognized all too clearly. Alderman felt a curious harmony of the spirits as he pulled the trigger, and watched with great satisfaction as the famous sachem stumbled and fell a few yards in front of him, his eyes filled with surprised mortality.

"Lordy, that was a might close for me," Cook stammered at Alderman as he went up and turned over the body to make certain the Indian was dead. Only when he saw the badly scarred hand did Cook realize who it was.

"Lordy, Lordy, Lordy," he said in hushed disbelief. "It's him, isn't it? It's King Philip." He looked at Alderman who, feeling in full harmony with the world, nodded his modest acknowledgement.

"Well, the Lord be praised," Cook said in awed tones as he gazed on the open eyes of the man he believed to be the Devil incarnate. "I guess it's finally over."

Plymouth - June, 1696

His father had spoken to him often of that terrible war, when the Indians had risen and tried to drive off the good people of New England. Horrible tales were told and retold by men now growing old. It seemed Boston was full of such men, and women too. But they meant little to young Moses Cook. He couldn't imagine that the towns he knew and visited often, like Marlboro and Lancaster, or even Brookfield, where his older sister Meg now lived, could have been a place where people were killed by Indians. The only Indians he knew were bent over old men who walked through the streets of Boston chanting prayers taught to them by some long forgotten missionary. The frontier was over a hundred miles to the west, and Moses could not imagine it ever being any closer.

Still the stories his father told thrilled him. They were exciting and romantic, much better than the dry lessons and even more remote Bible stories that were drilled into his head by both his head master and his minister. He never tired of hearing his father talk of Muttawmp and Matoonas, Weetamoo and Canonchet, One-Eyed John and Quinnapin.

But his favorite stories were of King Philip, the crafty old sachem who was present at every battle, riding a huge black horse, untouched by bullets even in the most terrifying of battles. In Moses' eyes, King Philip was more than a mere mortal. He was a dark angel, spreading fear and death before him. It was when he had told this to his father that this trip had been arranged.

His father drove their wagon through the crowded town streets, where chickens still squawked and ran from under the wagon's wheels as they rolled through. Plymouth was a bustling town, but not nearly as large as Boston, and Moses couldn't believe that back in the war Plymouth had been considered

Boston's equal. Moses watched a pig desperately try to make its way safely across the street under them.

Moses leaned over the wagon's rough board seat, trying to keep the pig in sight, when he felt it jolt to a halt and his father's hand pull him back up by the belt.

"There," his father said quietly. "There it is. Look."

Moses looked at the pole sticking in the ground in the town square in front of them and up at its top, fifteen feet off the ground. There a skull, bleached white from long years in the sun and rain, grinned on endlessly. Moses stared at the skull, fascinated.

"You mean it's been here all these years?"

"Yes."

"Why, father? Why have they kept his head here? For twenty years?"

Cook thought back a moment, to the war, the battles, to the nightmare that had engulfed the small colonies so early on in their growth.

"To prove he's dead, mainly," he finally said, picking up the reins and urging the horse forward. "And to show that he was a just a man. Back then no one believed it either. And if you listen to the old veteran's talk now, you'd still think he wasn't. But in the end that's all he was. Just a man."

As they rode off, Moses stared back at the skull still staring out across the town of Plymouth, the town King Philip had promised to push into the sea. It saddened Moses to know Philip's remains were there, in an open town square. After all, he'd been a huge historical figure, more important even, judging from the stories he heard, than David in the Bible.

"Why isn't he buried, father?" Moses finally asked. "Shouldn't he be buried somewhere else? Why isn't he buried in his own country?"

Cook said nothing in reply.

The End

Historical and Other Notes

Very little detail is known about King Philip and his life beyond the broad outlines, and much of this novel is an attempt to fill in those gaps within the known record. Motives and thoughts, especially when dealing with Metacomet, are within the realm of the novelist. His advisor Charles is a literary fiction.

The actual battles of King Philip's war are taken from firsthand accounts of the battles. The names of the participants, both Algonquin and English when known, are used, although details have been added as necessary. But these are meant to fill in, not to reshape. A basic guideline is, the more outlandish a detail, the more likely it is one based on the historical record.

Also a special thanks to my son, Nate, for helping to type large portions of this manuscript.

Made in the USA
Middletown, DE
01 January 2023

20891473R00089